"I'm onto you," *Shannon told his mother.*

"What?"

"Don't act innocent. You're trying to set me up again. I told you, I don't need help finding someone."

"How else am I supposed to get grandchildren?"

"If that's all you want, go adopt one."

"Well that defeats the purpose, doesn't it, if I can't return them at the end of the day."

"Really, Ma?"

"I am the only one of my friends without a daughter-in-law or grandchildren; and at the rate you're going, I'm going to see your father before I see any of that."

"Do you really think that I'd be attracted to any of these women?"

"I'm just giving you options."

"Ma, please just stop."

The older woman smiled, but neither confirmed nor denied what she would or would not be doing. This had him worried. If she had used a party to set him up with someone—anyone—what would she do to reach her objective? She was a stubborn woman and if she had her way, he would be married by the following year…which wasn't such a terrible idea, as long as it was to Joya.

Other Books By The Author

After The Call

Full of Grace

Speak Tenderly To Her

Stay With Me

Stepmother's Anonymous

The Best Love

THE BOOK OF JOY

Ruth E. Griffin

Studio Griffin
A Publishing Company
www.studiogriffin.net

THE BOOK OF

For my mother-in-law
Mearlin Jean Griffin

My heart is ever at your service.
William Shakespeare

And now, my daughter, fear not.
I will do for you all you require, for all my
people in the city know that you are a
woman of strength.
Ruth 3:11 (Amplified Bible, Classic Edition)

One

EVELYN BARTON REECE DID not consider herself a nosy neighbor. She was curious, concerned even, but not nosy. So, when she heard the sound of a school bus coming to a stop at the end of her street, she knew something was off. She paused the telephone conversation she was having with her friend Gail, then marched over to the window to investigate. There were several children in the neighborhood, ranging from kindergarten to high school. Most of the older kids rode the bus home, none of the younger ones did.

As a concerned neighbor, she knew this.

"Hold on," Evelyn advised her friend, as she reached the window, a little out of breath. As a septuagenarian, she had long passed the prime of her life. She had also passed her ideal weight decades earlier and was on the heavier side of the scale. However, a person only lived but so long, and life—and food— had to be enjoyed. This was the maxim she lived by and damn, if it hadn't led to a good, enjoyable life.

"What's wrong?" she heard Gail say, but Evelyn gave no response. She pulled aside the curtain and watched as the school bus opened its door. She didn't see anyone get off, but then the kids were small, and her eyes weren't as sharp as they used to be. Still, just to be on the safe side, she waited until the bus drove off before deciding nothing was wrong. It was then she spied a young girl, about five years of age, skipping to her house. Evelyn recognized her as the daughter of the new neighbor she had only briefly met. She thought it odd that the mother, who worked full-time, would be home at this hour, but Evelyn wasn't keen to her schedule. Still, she continued watching and found her curiosity was justified when the little girl walked up to her front door and turned the knob, only to discover it was locked. She tried the side door but found no one was home. Perplexed by the situation, the little girl just stood there.

"Gail, I'm gonna have to call you back," Evelyn said. Without waiting for a response, she hit the off button on the phone and set it on the table. Then she lumbered to the door and opened the screen far enough so that she didn't have to venture too far out. It wasn't officially summer yet, but the days were hot, and sticky.

"Hey," she yelled out, trying to get the little girl's attention, but to no avail. The girl continued staring at her house, as if trying to will someone to open the door.

"Hey, little girl," Evelyn called again, a little louder this time, as she swatted a fly attempting entry into her house. "Little girl!"

The child finally looked over towards her.

"Come here," Evelyn yelled, impatiently waving her hand towards her.

Still, the girl hesitated.

Evelyn let out a noisy sigh. She knew she wasn't making a very inviting impression on the girl, but she couldn't leave her standing out there by herself.

"Come here, child," she said with more force in her voice.

The girl vacillated for a moment longer before finally deciding to walk over. She cut through the adjacent neighbor's yard and arrived at Evelyn's doorstep in no time.

"What's your name, child?" the older woman asked.

"Hannah Myers," she replied, matter-of-factly. She squinted as she looked up at Evelyn. She was a beautiful girl, with large, round, curious eyes and black, curly hair that fell onto her face. Though her skin was the color of rich caramel, much lighter than Evelyn's dark brown tone, her features—nose, hair texture—were that of a black child. Mixed parentage, the older woman figured, no different than her son, Jackie.

"What are you doing home?" Evelyn

demanded, getting back to the topic at hand. "You don't normally catch the bus."

With an attitude befitting someone much older than her, Hannah placed her hands on her hips and replied, "I wanted to come home."

Evelyn glared back at her, surprised to hear such a tone come out of a small package.

"But you don't get to decide that, especially when your mother isn't home," she said.

"Well, I didn't want to go to after-school," Hannah returned, her eyes fixed on Evelyn, almost daring her to argue.

Evelyn marveled at her gumption. She had never met such a strong-willed child in her life and wasn't sure if she should be annoyed or impressed. Still, there was no excuse for the youngster to go out on her own and as the little girl's elder and neighbor, Evelyn had a responsibility to make sure Hannah was safe. She swung open the door to allow the little girl entrance.

"Come on in."

Hannah hesitated.

"What now?" Evelyn asked.

"I'm not supposed to go with strangers."

The child was strong-willed and smart—probably too smart for her own good.

"Well, I'm not a stranger, I'm your

neighbor."

"I don't know your name."

"Evelyn," she replied and extended her hand.

Hannah took hold of it and shook it.

"Now come inside before I get a house full of bugs," Evelyn insisted. Hannah didn't hesitate this time and entered. She had never been in the house before, but it didn't stop her from walking around like she knew where she was going. Evelyn stared at her curiously before closing the front door and following her into the kitchen.

"Can I have a snack?" Hannah asked, gazing up at the refrigerator.

Humored by the little girls' forwardness, Evelyn replied, "Sure. Have a seat."

The little girl removed her backpack and promptly obeyed. While Evelyn made her a sandwich (peanut butter and honey, as requested), Hannah peppered her with questions.

"Why is your hair white? Why do you have hair on your chin? Why is your house so old? Do you have any pets? Do you have any kids I can play with? Can I have some juice?"

Apparently, they were all rhetorical, because she kept right on talking.

"You look like my Grandma Wilma. She doesn't have white hair, but she's brown like you. Grandma Margery is peach like my mommy, not brown like you, and sometimes I stay with her when Mommy is working. She doesn't like my daddy. She said he's a loser and she's glad he's gone, but she likes Grandma Wilma, who calls me a lot and sends me letters in the mail. I'm going to see her in the summer. I'm gonna fly in an airplane and I'm gonna have fun with her. Can you cut my sandwich in half like my mommy does? It tastes better like that…"

Hannah was not a shy child; and Evelyn was enjoying her company, even if it was accidental…which reminded her.

"What's your mom's name?" Evelyn asked, finally able to get a word in edge-wise as Hannah started eating.

"Ashley Myers, but I'm not allowed to call her by her grown-up name—"

Evelyn interrupted her.

"Does your mom have a cell phone?"

"Yes. Sometimes she lets me play on it—"

Evelyn had to cut her off again.

"Alright sweetie, do you know her number? We need to call her to let her know you're here."

"She made me memorize it in case I got separated from her," Hannah stated, then gave Evelyn the number. While the little girl continued eating, Evelyn dialed. A young woman's voice greeted her.

"Are you Hannah's mom?" Evelyn asked.

There was a pause, followed by a sigh.

"What happened now?"

Evelyn reintroduced herself, then explained why she was calling. The woman immediately went from hesitant to frantic. She thanked Evelyn profusely and promised to leave immediately to pick-up her daughter.

"Don't rush and get yourself into an accident. She's fine. Just eating now, so take your time."

"I don't want to trouble you any further."

"Nonsense. It's no trouble. I don't mind the company. An old woman like me doesn't get too many visitors."

"Thank you, Ms. Evelyn."

"You're welcome," the older woman said and hung up. Then she sat down opposite of Hannah and listened as the little girl continued talking. The topics varied, but not her enthusiasm. She was energetic and animated as she talked. Evelyn couldn't help but smile. She didn't have grandchildren of her own, but she imagined this is what it would be like—talking, having fun, enjoying each other's company. Hannah was a good fill-in for right now, but oh, what joy that would be, if she had her own granddaughter.

Unfortunately, at the rate Jackie, her only child, was going, Evelyn was never going to realize that dream. He was fifty-years-old and though he was still young in her eyes, he was older than most single men out there looking for a potential spouse. At this point, Evelyn was happy to give up her old-fashioned standards if he chose to simply procreate. Regrettably, he wasn't even willing to do that. It wasn't fair to the child, he told her, to the mother or to him. Apparently, Evelyn and her husband had done *too* good of a job raising him…

Dammit, she thought.

The doorbell rang.

"Mommy!" Hannah shrieked and jumped up from the table.

"Hold on, Missy," Evelyn stated, pulling Hannah's attention back to her. She held her hand out to the little girl and said, "Here, help me up and we'll go see who's at the door together, okay?"

Hannah complied and took her hand. Evelyn stood up, her old back creaking and cracking in various places. Together they walked to the door, Hannah still holding onto her hand. Evelyn's heart melted a little.

"Mommy!" the little girl shrieked again when Evelyn opened the door.

A young woman stood there, a frenzied

look on her face. She hugged her daughter then asked, "What were you thinking getting on that bus?"

"I was ready to go home," Hannah replied matter-of-factly.

The woman sucked in a deep breath and through gritted teeth, said, "We'll talk about it when we get home. Where's your bookbag?"

"In the kitchen. I'll get it," the little girl stated and ran off to get it.

Evelyn smiled as she watched her go.

"Thank you again," Ashley said to the older woman. "Hannah's always had a strong will. It gets her in trouble and keeps me busy."

"It's alright, child. I'm glad to have helped out. And listen, if you need someone to watch her, just call me. You have my number now. Not too often, I'm an old woman, but I'll do what I can."

Ashley offered an appreciative grin then focused on Hannah as she came bounding back into the living room.

"Did you thank Ms. Evelyn?" her mother asked her.

Hannah grabbed Evelyn around the waist and hugged her.

"Thank you, Ms. Evelyn. See you later," she said, nonchalantly, as if their visit had been a planned one. Then she left, skipping alongside her mom as they walked to their house.

Evelyn felt good for having helped, but as she closed the door, she couldn't help the ache that crept into her heart. She wanted to believe she could still become a grandmother, but the truth was, with circumstances being what they were, it was much too late for that.

Yeah, right, Evelyn chuckled to herself as she wandered back into the kitchen. There might be an ache in her heart, but as long as there was breath in her body, it was never too late.

Two

"WHAT'S WRONG?" GAIL Evans asked again into the receiver. She got only silence though. "Evelyn?"

The line went dead. Gail blew out a noisy breath then hung up the phone. Evelyn was flighty in her younger years, but it seemed she had only gotten worse in her later ones. The two met at a community function as young women and became fast friends. There was something about Evelyn that drew Gail to her. She lived her life without apology, but more than that, she was an advocate for the underdog, and quick to make room for others, something she did for Gail often. Everyone loved her for it, especially her husband Jack.

Gail chuckled as she thought about him. Jack Reece was a down-to-earth, country boy—a *white* down-to-earth country boy— who fell in love with the dark-skinned beauty the first time he laid eyes on her. Evelyn had no plans to be tied down to anyone, much less a farmer whose experience of the world consisted of poker games in the back room of a general store, but there was something about this simple man that intrigued her.

Even knowing there was no way Jack's family would ever accept a woman like her, she still opted to pursue a relationship with him. Several months in, without waiting on the blessings of their families, the two married. Never mind the naysayers or racists who said they had no business being together—they decided they were going to prove the world wrong and live their own lives.

Gail, for her part, wasn't that brave, nor did she have to be. She married her high school sweetheart Earnest and devoted her life to him. Indeed, the roughest part about being with him was losing him too early. She had her son, Michael, but he had enlisted in the military and spent months, even years, deployed. For a time, Gail felt as if she had been left alone in the world. Then Michael married Joya, a beautiful Latin woman, who was everything Gail could have hoped for in a daughter-in-law—sweet, loving, hopeful, and loyal to a fault. He was stationed abroad and moved his wife and mother with him. The three became a tight-knit little family and life was back to being easy.

Then Michael died in a training accident. Both women were devastated by the loss, but it seemed Joya bounced back quicker than she did. Gail suffered with depression for some time and allowed the younger woman to care for her. After a while, though, Gail opted to return to her hometown. Joya followed and the two made a home there, reconnecting with old friends and family. Or at least tried to. The move wasn't easy for Gail and it was her old friend who looked her up and reconnected with her. Evelyn was moving slower these days, evidence of her advanced age, and she was a widow, her beloved Jack having succumbed to a heart attack years earlier. But the woman was still fearless and still a force to be reckoned with. Or at least Gail hoped so. Evelyn wasn't acting like she was right now. The woman had hung up on her without a valid explanation, when she made it clear she had something important to discuss with her! Gail was too old be playing those games. Even though she was younger than Evelyn by a few years, she looked older. Her hair was just as white, and her deep mocha skin had faded into a muddy brown color that lacked the luster and tone of her youth. The years hadn't been kind to her.

At least she had Joya. Having the younger woman around made life easier…

And there it is again, Gail thought, the word she was always looking for: easy. She wanted life to be easy. She wasn't naïve or stupid—she knew life would bring pain and hardships. But it had parceled out more than her share and it wasn't fair. Even if she had to deal with the bad parts, she just wanted things to go easy for a while, that's all.

Gail sighed, replaced the phone on the cradle, and grabbed the arm of the couch to help her stand. *Getting old is not for the faint of heart*, she thought. Her back seemed to ache in a different spot every time she got up, her joints were often stiff and her muscles constantly sore. What she wouldn't give to be twenty—even ten—years younger.

Finally on her feet, Gail shuffled into the kitchen to make herself some tea. Evelyn would eventually call her back whenever she was done doing what she had hung up on her to do, but Gail hoped it would happen *before* Joya got home. She was the topic of conversation; and knowing Joya the way she did, the younger woman would not be happy to know what she wanted to discuss. In fact, Joya would probably fight it. So, it was best she not know. As long as Evelyn delayed though, this wasn't going to happen. Then Joya would never get the happily ever after she deserved.

Gail busied herself with her tea and sat back down on the couch to watch her soaps. She was never one for daytime television when she was younger. Now as an older woman though, she found the stories distracting—exactly what she needed at this point in her life.

Unfortunately, they weren't distracting enough. She kept peering up at the clock on the wall, watching the minutes pass, anxious that Joya would be home soon. She was an elementary school teacher and didn't often stay too late. And with today being the last day of school, Gail expected her to walk through the door any time now.

The phone rang. Gail picked it up after the first ring, relieved to hear it was Evelyn.

"Where'd you go?" she demanded, flustered.

"I had to rescue my neighbor."

Evelyn proceeded to tell her about a little girl in her neighborhood. Gail half-listened to her friend's tale, rolling her eyes when words like 'life-saver' and 'hero' were strategically injected into the story.

"Is she okay now that you've saved the day?" Gail asked, her tone unmistakably sarcastic. "Can we talk about something else, like the reason I called you in the first place?"

Evelyn tsked.

"You've gotten grumpy in your old age," she said.

"And you've become flighty."

"No, that's license right there. I choose to

be flighty, because it keeps everyone around me on their toes. They don't know what to expect."

Gail couldn't argue with that logic. Instead, she opted to change the topic.

"Listen, is Shannon seeing anyone?" she asked, referring to Evelyn's son. The man's given name was Shannon, but it seemed everyone in the family had a different nickname for him, including his mother who called him Jackie.

"I don't think so. But then he doesn't talk to me about those things anymore. He thinks I talk too much and ask to many questions about his personal life and that I try to guilt him into getting married and giving me grandkids. Like I didn't give birth to him and he doesn't owe me his life or something."

A simple 'I don't know' would have sufficed for Gail but Evelyn was never one to take the short route anywhere.

"Is he looking?"

"Again, I don't know," Evelyn replied. Then she took in a sharp breath, as if she suddenly realized where Gail was going with her line of questioning. This was good—she needed Evelyn to do what Evelyn did and if she had to explain things repeatedly, her plan might not work. "What did you have in mind?"

"Well…what do you think of Joya?"

"What do you mean, what do I think of her? She's a sweetheart. The girl has a heart of gold. She will make some lucky man a wonderful wife…oh, I see where you're going with this. Is she aware of this conversation?"

Gail glanced up at the clock.

"No, but she might be if we don't finish up. She's supposed to be home soon."

"Okay, okay. So, what'd you have in mind? What brought this on?"

Gail had anticipated this question and practiced her response, not willing to delve into the truth quite yet.

"Look, we're two old bitties farting around, waiting to die. Joya is still young. She shouldn't be taking care of an old woman. She needs a husband and children to care for. And I've known Shannon most of his life. He's a good man in need of a good woman. I thought maybe the two of them would be good for each other."

"Well speak for yourself on the farting around bit, but I do agree with you."

"Do you think he would find Joya attractive?"

"If I was younger and played for the other team, *I'd* find Joya attractive."

"I didn't ask that," Gail retorted.

"I'm just saying. She's a beautiful

woman. In any case, he's all male. Of course, he will."

"Good, good. I was worried maybe that he was…you know…"

"What?"

"I thought since he hadn't gotten married in all these years that maybe he was…gay…," Gail said, struggling even with the word. She was painfully old-fashioned sometimes and struggled to understand things like sexual orientation and gender differences outside of the male and female variety. She just wanted things to go back to the way they used to be, when things were easy…

And there we go again…

"Are you kidding? No!" Evelyn exclaimed. "A mother has a sense about these things."

"Are you sure?"

"Gail, do you want to do this or not?"

"Yes. I just want to be sure Joya will be in good hands."

"What the hell is that supposed to mean?"

There was a hint of suspicion in Evelyn's voice. Gail cringed at her choice of words.

"I only meant that I want to be sure he's not harboring any secret desires for … you know, the manlier type. Because Joya's not…that."

"It's a good match, trust me."

"Alright. So, what are we going to do?"

"Leave that up to me," Evelyn said, taking charge of the situation, just as Gail hoped she would. "You just follow my lead, okay?"

"Alright."

Gail listened as Evelyn detailed her plan. Apparently, it was something she had given quite a bit a thought to before. This was good for Gail, as she didn't have the first clue about how to go about matching Shannon and Joya; and when she got off the phone with her friend, she felt a weight had been lifted off her. Evelyn might be impulsive and erratic; but she was also stubborn and determined. She was going to make sure Shannon and Joya found love. which was all Gail needed to hear. She would do her part, and when it was all said and done, she could rest knowing Joya wouldn't be left alone.

Three

SHANNON REECE WALKED INTO his office, placed his files onto his desk and dropped into his chair. Then he closed his eyes and took a deep breath. It had been a long day and he still wasn't done. He had a five-minute reprieve then he had to dial into a conference call, followed by a dinner meeting with a client. But such were his responsibilities now that he was a managing partner in the firm. It was a recent promotion that came with the usual perks—his name on the door, his own assistant and a corner office, as well as an increased workload. Shannon wasn't complaining; he was proud of his accomplishments and enjoyed his work. He was just tired.

Shannon took another deep breath and prepared to head out to his next meeting when his mobile phone rang. He dug it out of his pocket and saw it was his mother calling—again. He sighed. He wasn't in the mood to talk to her now, but he had already missed her previous two phone calls. If he didn't take it, he would risk her showing up at the office.

"Hi Ma," he said.

"Hey Jackie," she said, sweetly.

Shannon shook his head—he was fifty years old and she still called him by his nickname.

"How are you? Are you okay?" he asked her.

"Of course. Does something have to be wrong for me to call my son?"

"You called me three times."

"You didn't answer the first two."

"I was working."

"You're always working."

Her usual argument, he thought. But Shannon was unwilling to get into this discussion now.

"What do you want, Ma?"

"I'm just checking up on my favorite son."

"I'm your *only* son."

"Which makes you my favorite."

Shannon rolled his eyes and considered hanging up. She was a talker and could carry the conversation in circles if left unchecked. Of course, if he did hang up on her, she would definitely find her way to the office and embarrass him. He was stupid enough to test her on it once when he was in school and she showed up and fussed at him. He was humiliated. But that episode would pale in comparison if she showed up at his job to hassle him. He wasn't going to make that mistake again. Instead, Shannon settled for the direct route, even knowing it wouldn't work.

"Listen, if there's nothing, I have to get ready for my next meeting, which I'm running late for—"

"What happened with Trina?"

The question threw him off. Trina was his ex-girlfriend. What was his mom up to?

"We broke up. Last year," he replied, not even trying to hide the suspicion in his voice. "Is that why you called me?"

"Why did you and Trina break up?" she asked, ignoring his question.

"Why does it matter? You didn't like her anyway."

"I didn't?"

"No."

"Why?"

Shannon sighed, loudly. He didn't want to rehash this, especially over the phone.

"Because of her line of work."

"Oh. Was she the dominatrix?"

"Yes," Shannon replied, remembering the brief encounter between them. Both women were polite enough, but Evelyn couldn't get past the woman's chosen career, which led to a myriad of questions that Shannon was not prepared for.

Is that the kind of things you're into? Getting

tied up and having a woman tell you want to do? Shoot, that's marriage. You should just get married if that's what you're into. Does she have sex with her clients? Does she have an office she goes to where men pay her to do this? Does she do this with women? Equal rights and all that, right? Seriously, though, what kind of man likes to be dominated by women. I mean, your dad was more of the relaxed kind of guy, but in the bedroom…

Shannon cringed, trying to block out the rest of the conversation. Trina's profession didn't bother him. She didn't advertise what she did and certainly didn't bring her work home with her. But knowing his mother's persistent nature, it was just easier to be alone than try to continue the relationship.

"Oh." Evelyn paused and seemed ready to drop the subject…but of course, she didn't. "Well, are you seeing anyone else?"

Shannon sighed. He wasn't going to win.

"I really do have to go."

"Alright, alright. Are you coming over tonight? I made dinner."

"I already have dinner plans but thank you."

"Well, don't forget the party this weekend then."

Shannon closed his eyes and rubbed his temple. He couldn't forget if he tried. His mom had always been a social person, and age hadn't done much to slow her down. It was at a party that his parents met, and though his father was more low-key and preferred an evening at home, he didn't discourage his wife's affinity for socializing. Indeed, Ms. Evelyn Reece was known for her parties—Spring Celebrations, Christmas Affairs, Fourth of July Parties, etc. In fact, summer wasn't summer without her official kick-off. And as her son, it was his responsibility to make sure his mother had everything she needed…to party.

"Someone's gotta keep you out of trouble," he responded, tongue-in-cheek, but also serious.

She didn't pick up on it.

"You remember Gail, don't you?" she asked.

How could he not remember her? She was his mother's oldest friend, which automatically made her like an aunt to him. It had been some time since they saw each other, but that didn't change their status as family.

"Yes, I remember Gail. How's she doing?"

"She's doing fine. I talked with her today—she'll be coming to the party. She and her daughter-in-law, Joya. So are your cousins on your daddy's side, and my side as well. And your uncle Otis. Oh, and I also invited my new neighbor. She's got a daughter, precious thing, I think you'll like them. And you know we got a new mailman. Actually, it's a woman, so ..."

Shannon didn't hear a word after she mentioned the name 'Joya'. Something like an electric spark ran through him for a moment as he remembered the first time he saw her, earlier in the year. Standing at about five feet to Shannon's six-foot frame, Joya Evans was nothing short of stunning. She was in her early thirties, of Latin descent with bronze-colored skin and eyes the color of rich chocolate. Her dark, wavy hair covered her shoulders and she was proportionately curvy. And if looks weren't enough, she had a thoroughly positive, engaging and genuine personality.

They saw each other only a handful of times in the past few months, but Shannon couldn't help but appreciate Joya even more each time. Even after Michael's death, Joya remained positive and loving. Shannon convinced himself that it was respect he was feeling, but the more he thought about her, the more he was sure that he was crushing on what was essentially his kin's widow.

Aren't you too old to be acting like that?

It's her youthfulness making you feel young

again.

Nope, that's wrong.

You're appreciating Michael's choice in spouse?

That's even worse.

Appreciating her beauty?

Give it up. She's probably still grieving.

Indeed, it had only been a year since Michael's accident, and though Joya was optimistic and encouraging there was a certain sadness about her that made him wonder—and also put her out of arm's reach.

Disappointed with his train of thought, Shannon returned his focus to his mother, who continued rambling on, though Shannon was unsure about what.

"…a woman from church, Tammy. Beautiful girl. Well, she is on the inside. Outside she's a little plain, but you always say you don't look at the skin-deep features. Plus, she's a dentist, which technically means she's a doctor. Oh, and Martha's daughter, Stacey, will be there. You remember her, from Sunday school? She's going through a divorce, but she tells me the marriage has been over for a while now. There's also Leigh and Paige—they're twins. You might have seen them on television, they were contestants on that singing show—"

"What?" Shannon interrupted, confused.

Evelyn paused briefly, then innocently said, "What, what?"

"What are you talking about?"

"I was just telling you who I invited."

Shannon thought about the names he heard and decided the guest list sounded suspiciously one-sided. He wasn't vain enough to believe his mother would try to use her party to set him up with someone, but the truth was, she just hadn't done it *yet*. She posted ads on his behalf, signed him up for dating websites, and invited women over for dinner. Was it so hard to believe that she would use her party as another means for him to meet someone?

Shannon shook his head incredulously, even as Evelyn continued rattling off names. Though he was a successful attorney, the first in his family to finish college and be named partner in a successful firm, his mother had a way of making him feel like a failure for not getting married and having a family. Indeed, his life hadn't gone according to plan in that department, but it wasn't for lack of trying. He had had several serious relationships, had even been engaged once before, but things didn't work out with his intended. So what if he was fifty years old and still a bachelor? Shannon was happy with that.

Or he thought he was, until he talked to

his mother and she undid everything he had worked so hard to do.

Of course, if he was completely honest, it wasn't until he met Joya that his life truly became undone and he began to wonder if it couldn't use a little Latin spark in it.

Be real. What would she want with an old man like you anyway?

Shannon decided he was done with the entire conversation—and not just the parts where he was chastising himself. He cut his mother off in mid-sentence (something about inviting his coworkers).

"Ma, look, if there's nothing else, I've gotta go—"

"What do you mean, if there's nothing else?"

There was a knock on his door, followed quickly by Nathan Withers sticking his head into his office. The man was a senior partner in the firm, and his friend. He had been instrumental in Shannon's promotion, making him the only non-white partner. Nathan insisted it was his talent that got him where he was, but Shannon understood having Nathan's support also helped. And he appreciated him for it.

"I'll see you Saturday, okay?" Shannon said to his mother and then hung up. He tried not to think about the implications of his actions and quickly slipped his phone into his pocket. He turned his attention to Nathan, who asked, "Are you ready, Reece? We're gonna be late."

"Yeah," Shannon said, reaching for his portfolio. "Yeah, I was just regrouping."

Nathan opened the door wider and stood in the door way, waiting for him. The man was about his age, still fit, still handsome—a silver fox, Shannon had heard the women in the office say. But the man was a confirmed bachelor, enjoying the company of many women instead of one. Indeed, he loved playing the field and often encouraged Shannon to follow his example, even setting him up on blind dates.

It seemed everyone in Shannon's life had a say about his dating status—or lack thereof.

"Who was that?" Nathan asked.

"My mother. She's doing her yearly start-of-summer-party thing on Saturday and was just running over the guest list with me," Shannon replied as he approached the door. He wasn't one to lie, but when he saw Nathan perk up, he instantly knew he should have. "No, I'm not inviting you," Shannon groaned.

"Come on," his friend pleaded. "Her parties are legendary."

"I had to rebuild the front porch after the

last one."

"Exactly."

Shannon stopped and stared at his friend. The man was holding his hands in front of him, begging for an invitation.

"Are you serious?"

"You're not someone unless Ms. Evelyn Reece invites you to one of her parties."

"This isn't even one of her bigger ones. It's just a small get-together."

"Beggars can't be choosers," Nathan replied, almost giddy at the prospect of going.

Shannon shook his head in disbelief and walked off.

Four

JOYA EVANS FINISHED UP HER paperwork and sat back, tired. Despite the challenges that came with teaching five- and six-year-olds, she enjoyed her job. Even on days like this one, when the kids were more rambunctious than usual. However, it was the last day of school, so their behavior could be excused. After spending the day watching videos and playing games, they were anxious to leave. Joya should have been too, but with the prospect of summer ahead of them, she was dreading the thought of being by herself for the next couple of months. After her husband Michael passed away, she found it difficult to be on her own. All she thought of was him and the gaping hole he left when he died. At least when she was focused on others she didn't have to think about how much she missed him.

"Hey Joya."

Joya turned around and saw one of the other first-grade teachers walking into her classroom. She was carrying a medium-sized box with her.

"Oh, hi Sarah," Joya said, standing up.

"I brought those books I was telling you

about. They should keep you busy over the summer."

"Thank you," Joya stated, as Sarah set the box on her desk and opened it. It was filled with books, ranging from romances to biographies. Sarah was the head of a book club and had invited her to be a part of it. While Joya welcomed the chance to participate, what she really wanted was the opportunity to get lost in another world, even if only for a little while.

"I'll send you an email with our schedule, rating system and everything else you'll need to know," Sarah said. "It'll be nice to have a reader in our group. Some of the ladies are just there to talk, which don't get me wrong, can be fun. But we're there to discuss books and…well, let's just say, sometimes we don't."

Joya picked up one of the larger books and flipped through it. It was a biographical novel, with lots of large words. Yes, this would work well.

"You're welcome to hang onto them as long as you want to," Sarah added. "My husband already thinks I have too many books."

Joya smiled. Michael used to say the same thing.

"Thank you. I look forward to joining

you guys."

"No problem," Sarah said, then added. "I'll see you next week."

Joya nodded. She packed up the box and finished up her work, so she could go home. The books would definitely help fill up the empty space. And she would also meet people and make new friends. But even with those prospects, Joya couldn't help but feel a twinge of sadness and anxiety for the summer ahead.

JOYA'S MIND was deep in thought when she walked in to her apartment, placed her keys on the hook by the door and dropped her bags on the floor.

"Joya, is that you?"

Gail's voice drew her to the present.

"Yes, ma'am," she replied, slipping off her shoes. She was ready to sit down and relax, when her mother-in-law appeared in the archway between the foyer and the hallway, dressed to go out. Joya cringed. "I'm forgetting something, aren't I?"

The older woman smiled sympathetically.

"We were gonna go shopping so I can get a new dress for Evelyn's party," she replied, then taking her in, added, "But we can cancel if you're too tired."

Joya remembered her promise.

"No, I'm not too tired," she lied, putting her shoes back on, "Just let me freshen up."

"Are you sure, baby? I know those children can wear you out," Gail insisted.

Joya let out a chuckle.

"I think it's more that I'm getting old," she replied.

Gail's smile turned to laughter, her rich, brown skin glowing younger than her sixty-plus years.

"If you're old, then I'm in trouble," she said.

Joya was happy to hear her laugh.

"We both are," she agreed then added, "I'll be right back."

She went to the bathroom and splashed some water on her face. She used a hand towel to dab it dry, then looked at her reflection. She thought of herself as pretty, but the exhaustion she felt lately was beginning to show. The bags underneath her eyes were pronounced, while her skin was devoid of its normal bronze radiance. She needed to get more sleep; and now that summer was here, perhaps she would.

Joya reapplied her make-up, brushed out her hair; and changed her clothes. Feeling presentable again, she found her mother-in-law.

"Ready?" she asked the older woman,

who was seated on the couch, waiting. She smiled and held her arm up for assistance. Joya helped her stand and together they left. She listened as Gail told her about her day, interrupting her mother-in-law only to let her know they had arrived at the mall. She helped the older woman out of the car and kept pace with her until they arrived inside the department store.

"So, who's going to be at the party?" Joya asked. She had met only a handful of Gail's friends and family members since moving into town, but it wasn't for lack of trying. Gail suffered with depression since the death of Michael and was resistant to reconnecting with old acquaintances or rekindling old friendships. Even her relationships with family suffered. She had a sister close in age and appearance whom she had been close to in their younger years, but now they didn't speak at all.

Gail was trying now though, as evidenced by her desire to attend Evelyn's party. This meant a lot to Joya. Maybe she was selfish in her reasoning, but her mother-in-law was all she had left in the world and if Gail gave up, Joya wasn't sure she could keep going.

"I don't know really. Evelyn's never met a stranger, so there's no telling who'll show up."

They wandered over to the woman's section of the store and started browsing through the racks. Joya noted how much slower Gail was moving. She had had a stroke years earlier, and though she made a full recovery, she sometimes had trouble getting around during the day. She also tired a lot easier. It took Gail a while to accept Joya's help and to rest when she needed it, but as a precaution, Joya learned to recognize any tell-tale symptoms, since Gail's chances for another stroke had increased after her first one.

"How's this?" Joya asked, holding up a sheer blouse with sequins.

The older woman smiled and shook her head.

"No one wants to see that much of this old body."

"Oh, I don't know. I think you're beautiful," Joya said, as she replaced the shirt. "I hope I look that good when I'm your age."

"You are being overly generous," Gail stated, and pulled out a brown, loudly-patterned, short-sleeved dress. "Too busy?"

Joya nodded.

"It's too dark. You need something spring-y. Maybe peach-colored and solid. No patterns."

They continued browsing in silence.

"Shannon will be there," Gail suddenly said.

Joya looked up at her, her thoughts elsewhere.

"Hmm?"

"Shannon. Evelyn's son. He'll be there."

Joya recalled him. He was tall and handsome; and a gentleman to boot. It was a rare combination that she had found in only one other man—Michael, who was everything her heart yearned for.

"It'll be nice to see him," she said almost absent-minded, then pulled out a soft-white, cotton dress and held it out to Gail. "I like this one."

Her mother-in-law nodded and said, "I'll try it on."

Joya followed her to the dressing room and waited while she tried it on. She came out after a few minutes, looking stunning.

"Like I said, beautiful," Joya said.

Gail smiled. She went back into the dressing room and changed back to her clothes. Then they paid for the dress and walked into the mall.

"So what else are we getting?" Joya asked.

"We have to get you something. You're coming too."

"I'm fine. I'm sure I've got something in the closet I can wear."

"You should get something nice for yourself. We're okay in our finances."

Joya put her arm around her mother-in-law and said, "We are. I just prefer to focus on you. Who knows, maybe you'll meet someone." She meant the comment to be tongue-in-cheek, and indeed, they had joked around in the past about finding someone for Gail. But whereas the older woman would smile ruefully once upon a time, today her smile disappeared altogether. "Are you okay?" Joya asked her.

"Let's sit," Gail said.

Joya maneuvered the older woman to a vacant bench and helped her sit.

"Are you okay?" she asked again.

Joya figured she had expended too much energy and needed to rest. But her mother-in-law took a deep breath, connected eyes with her and said, "Baby, you know it'd be okay with me if you found someone, right?"

Joya frowned. Where was this coming from? Because she joked around?

"What are you talking about?"

"You were a loyal and loving wife to Michael. But he's gone, and I want you to live your life to the fullest."

Joya didn't know what to say. The words were a surprise, especially coming from Gail. So soon after Michael's death too. Was she feeling down again?

Or was Joya wearing her emotions on her

sleeve?

"I know you do," Joya finally said.

"Michael wouldn't want you to be alone."

Joya's eyes stung with unshed tears, but she wouldn't let them fall. She blinked them away and smiled for Gail. She took her mother-in-law's hand and kissed it.

"I'm not alone. I've got you."

Gail glared at her but didn't say anything for the longest time. Finally, she offered her daughter-in-law a small smile and said, "Let's get some dinner."

Five

SHANNON PULLED INTO THE driveway of his mother's two-story gabled house and put his car in park. He looked around at all the cars lining the street and debated whether he really wanted to get out or not. The party had already started, which made him fashionably late, but being the son of Evelyn Barton Reece, it was expected that he should be. He had stopped by the previous evening to help with the set-up and to drop off all the supplies she needed, but it was all habit at this point. His mother had been doing this his entire life, getting people together to celebrate whatever was on the agenda that day. Holidays, of course, and birthdays, but there were also anniversaries, memorials, seasonal and solar events. Truth be told, his mother never needed much of an excuse to party. And given her advanced age, Shannon didn't hold it against her. She had buried her husband and much of her family; and whatever time she had left, Shannon wanted her to enjoy life.

Of course, that left him to referee her little ho-downs and put things back together when she was done. But it was worth it…or so he told himself.

Shannon turned off his car and exited the vehicle. He could hear music blaring and could see a handful of people loitering on the front porch and around the back gate, but most seemed to be congregated in the backyard. The house was on several acres of land and though half of it was wooded, his mother could ideally host several hundred people. By the look of it, a good number had showed up to party. Shannon took the worn path to the house and climbed the familiar steps to the side door. They creaked and moaned with every step he took. Shannon loved the house; it was his childhood home, but it was beginning to show its age. Not just that, every party his mother hosted took its toll on the structure. He was exaggerating about having to rebuild the front porch, but only slightly. Though the gatherings were relatively tame compared to how they used to be, repairs still had to be made after one (or more) of the guests got a little too rowdy. If his mother wanted to continue living there, it had to be gutted out and rebuilt: the stairs in the basement, the back steps, the back porch, the roof, the ancient heater, the floors in the kitchen, the upstairs—everything. Shannon didn't want to get rid of the house, but he was pragmatic enough to understand the house was just wood, brick and plaster.

Old wood, brick and plaster in need of repair, he reminded himself. *Just like its owner.*

Of course, Shannon would never say that to his mother, but the allegory was not lost on him. They had aged together and even though both were still holding on, it was only a matter of time before they completely fell apart. But getting rid of the house was not his decision to make—it was his mother's and every time he brought the subject up, she stubbornly reminded him that this was the house his father built for her and she wasn't going to move. Which then left him with only one option: take care of immediate repairs and try to convince his mother that moving was in her interest.

Yeah right, Shannon told himself, as he walked into the house. That was never going to happen. Shannon shelved the internal conversation as he walked through the mudroom and entered the kitchen, where he found several women, huddled together by the sink, talking and laughing as they fixed plates. Shannon's uncle Otis, Ms. Evelyn's younger brother, grabbed a beer, then disappeared into the living room where he deposited himself in front of the television to watch a game. Two children about five or six years of age ran through the room, giving him a wide berth. Such was Shannon's usual experience at his mother's parties—Mr. Invisible—and he was happy to keep it that way. He was there for damage control, that was all.

"Well, hello there," a dark-skinned, middle-aged woman drawled as she approached him. She was short and curvy, wearing a skin-tight dress that left nothing to the imagination. Though she was very pretty, she smiled in a way that reminded Shannon of a predator playing with its prey.

"Hi," he said, cautiously. He didn't like the way she was sizing him up.

"I'm Carmella," she said as she leaned into him.

"Shannon," he introduced himself and leaned back.

"Sha-*nnon*," she reiterated, bringing her hand up to his chest. "You're just a handsome piece of caramel taffy, aren't you?"

Shannon shuddered.

"What do you do for a living?" she continued.

"I'm a lawyer," he replied, wondering why he didn't lie.

"Well now," she said and met his gaze. "Handsome *and* rich, huh?"

Shannon took a step around her and quickly said, "It was nice meeting you," before slinking away. He didn't look back, certain she would pounce on him if he did. He winced at the thought and walked into the living room to search for his mother. He found only his uncle.

"What's up man?" Otis said, though his attention was fixed on the television.

"You seen Ma?"

"Nope," he replied not once looking at him.

Shannon waited for another moment, hoping to get more from him, but Otis said nothing else. The man was focused, and Shannon was just a mere interruption.

Still invisible.

Shannon continued onto the family room, where there were a group of women drinking and laughing. He looked around briefly, hoping not to attract attention, but he hesitated too long at the doorway and one of the women saw him. Heads started popping up and within seconds, all the women were gazing at him. Shannon suddenly felt like he was on display.

"Oh, girl, look at who just walked in," one of the women said, rising to her feet. She was tall and thin and very drunk. Her gait was far from straight though and she tripped as she approached him. Without even thinking, Shannon reached out and caught her.

"Are you okay?" he asked her.

"I am now," she said, breathing heavily. She reeked of alcohol and garlic.

The other women in the room giggled. Two of them rose to check on the woman.

"Maybe you should sit down," he suggested, moving her towards an empty chair.

"Sit with me," she said. She smiled at him and raised her hand up to his face. He moved his head to avoid her touch. "You are fine," she added.

Shannon had a sudden urge to flee. He stood up and stepped back. One of the women followed him.

"I'm just looking for my mother, Ms. Evelyn Reece," he said.

"You're Evelyn's boy?" she asked.

"Yes."

"I'm Stacey," she said and offered him her hand. "Evelyn's talked a lot about you. So, what do you do, Evelyn's boy?"

"Have you seen my mom?" he asked, ignoring her question. Why was everyone so interested in his profession anyway?

"Not recently, but don't be in such a rush to leave. The party's just getting started."

"Thanks for the offer, but I really should go. Ladies," Shannon said and quickly left the room. Their laughter followed him down the hall. He couldn't help but wonder about the company his mother was keeping in her old age.

Shannon went outside, hoping for better luck. The backyard was teeming with life. People were gathered in bunches, dancing, eating, drinking, socializing. He recognized a couple of the neighbors and saw several family members over by the grill, but everyone else was a stranger to him. Shannon walked around until he found Evelyn sitting at a fold-out table with her friend Gail.

"Hey Ma," he said loudly to be heard over the music. She lit up when she saw him.

"Hey Jackie!"

She held up her arms and reached for him. He hugged her.

"Hi Auntie," he said turning to Gail and offered her a hug and kiss.

"Hey baby," she returned with a tight embrace.

He sat between them.

"Who are all these people?" he asked.

"Just some friends," his mother replied.

"From where?"

"Church."

He raised an eyebrow.

"These people go to church? With us?"

"Don't be so judgmental. Even Jesus hung out with prostitutes and tax collectors."

"Yeah, but he didn't supply them with

alcohol."

"Well, actually…"

Shannon groaned.

"Don't say it."

"…there was that one wedding."

Shannon sighed. He wasn't going to win an argument with his mother and rather than expend anymore energy trying, he turned to Gail.

"You let her do this?"

The older woman threw her hands up and shook her head.

"I had nothing to do with it," she replied. "No one lets—or stops—your mother from doing anything."

This was true, which meant they were just along for the ride.

"Alright," he sighed. "What do you need me to do?"

Evelyn sat back and smiled, as if the answer was an obvious one.

"You are so much like your father. Go get something to eat. Relax. Have fun."

She meant her words as a chastisement, but Shannon took them as a compliment. His father was the strongest, most influential man in his life and he was proud to be compared to him.

"Fine, Ma. Can I get either one of you anything while I'm up?" he asked.

Gail shook her head.

Evelyn said, "Get me some more punch, will you?"

Shannon grabbed her cup and stood up. Looking around the yard, he saw a refreshment table had been set up near the grill and he started in that direction, nodding and politely greeting the various guests he walked by. By his estimation, there had to be about over one hundred people loitering about—most of them women—and he had to squeeze by them to get to the punch. An older woman, probably about Gail's age, was holding the ladle to the punch bowl.

"Hey there cowboy, you need some help?"

She winked at him and blew him a kiss.

Shannon sighed. This was getting old.

"If you don't mind," he replied, holding out his mother's cup. The woman took it from him and drew out some punch.

"I'm Felicia," she said.

"Shannon."

"So how do you know Ms. Evelyn?"

"She's my mother."

"Oh, my goodness, I should have known—you look just like her," the woman gushed as she reached for a second filling. "She's mentioned you before. Said you were smart and handsome. You're so much better looking than she said."

Shannon smiled politely, unsure how to respond to that.

"Listen, I know we just met, but if you ever wanna kick it or something, I'm available," Felicia stated as she set the ladle down and turned back towards him. She smiled teasingly, took a sip from the cup and gave it back to him, her eyes still glued to him. Then she pulled a card from her brassiere and handed it to him. "Call me," she said and winked at him.

Shannon frowned, thoroughly disgusted with her actions. He turned around and walked away. Rather than return to the table though, he veered towards the house and into the kitchen, which thankfully had been vacated. He proceeded to pour the drink into the sink and throw the cup and the card away.

What the hell is wrong with these women?

Shannon washed his hands, feeling dirty from the encounter. After drying them, he reached into the cabinet for a clean glass when he heard the most angelic voice say his name. He turned around and his heart nearly stopped—it was Joya.

Six

"JOYA," SHANNON SAID, HIS tone sounding a little more surprised than he intended. Or perhaps just relieved.

"Shannon," she said, meeting him at the sink. Without any hesitation, she reached up and hugged him. Shannon's heart thumped with approval as he returned the hug. Joya released him all too soon and stepped back, a smile on her beautiful face. Standing so close to her, Shannon couldn't help but take in her scent. It filled his lungs and painted pleasant images of her in his mind. "It's good to see you," she added.

"You have no idea how happy I am to see *you*," he said truthfully. "These women here are scary."

She chuckled.

"Oh, stop," she waved at him, then moved to the counter, where she grabbed a bottle of water. "They're just a little lonely, that's all. Your mom was trying to help their group."

Shannon stopped, suspicious.

"What group?"

"It's a new singles group that meets at the same center where her senior's group meets for some of their classes. She was talking to them and invited them to the party, so they would have a chance to meet and mingle with other members of the community."

Church indeed. Everything made sense now and knowing his mother the way he did, she probably meant for them to meet and mingle *with him*. He shook his head and walked over to the table. Joya followed.

"So how did you get wrangled into all this?" he asked her, pulling out a chair for her.

"Thank you," she said with a smile. "I came with Ms. Gail. I wanted to make sure she was getting out and spending time with her friends. And to have fun too, but mostly for her."

"She's lucky to have you," he said taking a seat beside her.

"Nah. I'm lucky to have her," Joya said dismissively, then added, her tone lighter, "Besides, I'm off for the summer, so I'd probably be bored to tears if I wasn't here."

"That's right, you're a teacher, aren't you?"

"First-grade."

"How's that going?"

"I love it. The kids are great. Keeps me busy."

There was a momentary silence between them as Shannon found himself staring at Joya, admiring her lovely smile. He cleared his throat and said, "Well, I'm glad you're here," Shannon admitted. It was the first thing he thought of, but even as true as those words were, he felt the need to elaborate, because he couldn't have her thinking he liked her or something. Being around her made him feel like he was twelve years old again. "I'm not a party-person," he quickly added.

"Really? Because to hear your mother talk about you, one might be led to believe you were the most popular person on this planet."

He laughed.

"No, that would be her. I am happy to sit back and let her take the limelight. That's what my dad always did."

Joya smiled, knowingly.

"What?" he asked.

"It's just cute, thinking about your parents," she responded.

It took him a minute to understand what she meant.

"Oh, you mean the interracial thing."

"Yeah. I'm a little biased, but I think mixed couples are beautiful. As are their children."

As much as Shannon wanted to beam in her comment—*the possibilities*, his heart told him—he couldn't help but notice the sadness in her voice. Was she thinking about Michael? Or was there something else? Was it even his business to ask? Technically their relationship could be defined as friendship, but it was more of a friendship by default, like when one kid's mom was friends with another kid's mom and they spent time together, so the two kids had no choice but to hang out and be friends. Of course, he and Joya were adults so that didn't really apply, and he was older than her, but he liked to think that their relationship was real. All of this was moot though when he considered how much she affected him. There was something about Joya, beyond her physical beauty, that had his heart tied in knots. And for that reason, Shannon opted to change the conversation.

"Yeah. They lived in a different era

back then, but they made it work," he said, closing off the topic. "So, tell me, Joya, what is it you plan to do with your summer? I don't think I've had a summer off in decades."

Shannon regretted the comment—it dated him. The last thing he wanted her to think about was his age.

"I haven't decided yet," she said. "I've got a couple of weeks of work left, but beyond that, I've been thinking about maybe getting a part-time job or volunteering somewhere."

Uncle Otis wandered back into the kitchen just then. He didn't acknowledge them but kept his eyes on the television in the other room. His movements were mechanical as he opened the fridge, pulled out another can of beer and popped the lid. It was only after he took a sip that he asked, "You find your momma, Junior?"

"Yes sir."

Otis nodded, then walked back out. Joya turned to Shannon once he was gone.

"I have to ask…," she said and paused, as if waiting for him to give her permission. The wistfulness was gone from her voice, replaced with an infectious playfulness that had him smiling and wanting to tell her anything she desired to know.

"What?"

"Gail calls you Shannon, Ms. Evelyn calls you Jackie and your uncle just called you Junior…," she observed. "Why so many names?"

Okay, anything but that, he thought. Where his name was concerned, Shannon divulged little and told no one beyond human resources and medical providers. They were the only ones who needed to know his full name. However, because it was Joya asking, he would oblige. With a dramatic sigh his mother would have been proud of, Shannon said, "It's a complicated story, but if I tell you, I have to swear you to secrecy."

"Oh, that serious?"

"Very serious."

She raised her right hand.

"Consider me sworn."

Shannon cleared his throat.

"My grandfather on my dad's side was John Shannon Reece. Biggest, tallest, most fierce-some Irishman you ever met. Everyone called him Big John and aptly so. When my dad was born, his name, of course, was also John Shannon Reece, but everyone called him Jack in deference to my grandfather. When I came along, I was supposed to be a junior, like my dad. My mom had already determined that she was going to call me Jackie. Except the nurse who was attending my birth got the names mixed up and I ended up with Junior Shannon Reece."

Shannon paused, waiting for Joya to react. She only smiled, but he could see she was trying to contain her laughter.

"Go ahead, laugh," he said.

Her smile only got bigger.

"No, I think that's cute."

Because, yes, cute was what he was going for at his age. Though it wasn't the worst thing in the world…

"Why didn't your parents change it?" she asked.

He shrugged his shoulders.

"Too much red tape. Mistrust of government. They already called me Jackie and Junior, what was the point…you pick the reason."

"So, your driver's license, passport, all legal papers…"

He nodded.

"Junior Shannon Reece."

Joya let out a loud laugh, then quickly covered her mouth to stifle it. She cleared her throat and asked, "Why didn't *you* change it?"

He shrugged his shoulders again.

"By the time I got old enough to do it, my dad had passed, and it just didn't seem important anymore. I went by Shannon in college and just left it as it was."

"Well, I like your name," she said resolutely. "I think it fits you."

"And I think you're lying but thank you."

They continued talking for the better part of an hour, but Shannon paid no attention to the time, or the people who passed through the kitchen. He forgot about the party and let his thoughts center on Joya—her eyes, her smile, her body. Did she even know how beautiful she was? Most women did. Somehow though, he didn't think Joya knew, or cared. She was genuine, and Shannon couldn't help the ache that invaded his heart. *If only*…but the possibility that she might requite what he was feeling towards her seemed beyond impossible. She was Michael's wife—nay, his widow—and this was enough to shut down that conversation.

Eventually, Shannon said, "Ma's probably wondering where her punch is."

Joya stood up, a mischievous smile on her face.

"Well, come on. I'll protect you from the female predators out there."

Shannon laughed at the thought but had to get serious when they reached the refreshment table. Felicia was still there, and her countenance had changed from flirty to combative when she saw Joya at his side. He thought about how ugly it could quickly get and placed himself between the two women, just in case. Thankfully Felicia only sneered at him, then walked away. Shannon and Joya got drinks and food and walked back to where Evelyn and Gail were sitting. He set his plate and punch down, helped Joya take her seat, then joined everyone else.

"I thought I was going to have to send out a search party," Evelyn remarked.

"Yeah it was a regular wilderness out there," Shannon replied, glowering at his mother.

She smiled innocently.

Shannon couldn't help but wonder what it was exactly his mother was trying to accomplish. She wasn't really trying to set him up, was she? She had tried before, but her standards were a lot higher. By the look of the women around him, Evelyn was scraping the bottom of the barrel in desperation. He wasn't normally so critical or judgmental of others, but when compared to Joya...well, there was no comparison. No, Evelyn was up to something, he just didn't know what yet.

Gail pushed her chair back.

"Excuse me. Nature calls," she said.

"Do you need some help?" Joya asked her as she started to rise. The older woman nodded, then accepted help from her daughter-in-law. The two walked slowly towards the house, giving Shannon the opportunity he needed to confront his mother.

"I'm onto you," he told her.

"What?"

"Don't act innocent. You're trying to set me up again. I told you, I don't need help finding someone."

"How else am I supposed to get grandchildren?"

"If that's all you want, go adopt one."

"Well that defeats the purpose, doesn't it, if I can't return them at the end of the day."

"Really Ma?"

"I am the only one of my friends without a daughter-in-law or grandchildren; and at the rate you're going, I'm going to see your father before I see any of that."

"Do you really think that I'd be attracted to any of these women?"

"I'm just giving you options."

"Ma, please just stop."

The older woman smiled, but neither confirmed nor denied what she would or would not be doing. This had him worried. If she had used a party to set him up with someone—anyone—what would she do to reach her objective? She was a stubborn woman and if she had her way, he would be married by the following year…which wasn't such a terrible idea, as long as it was to Joya. However, since this wasn't a possibility, his mother needed to mind her own business.

Seven

"WELL, DID IT WORK?" Gail asked, her voice low since Joya was in the other room. It was early in the day, and Gail was sitting on her bed talking to Evelyn. The television was playing in the background, hopefully drowning out any part of the conversation Joya might hear. "Did Shannon say anything?"

"He said they were just friends, but you saw the way they were looking at each other, didn't you? And how long they were talking in the kitchen? They weren't swapping recipes, I can tell you that."

"So, what do we do now?"

"We keep the momentum going."

"Okay, but no more parties. Some of those people you invited looked more than a little suspicious."

Gail wasn't the extrovert that her friend was, but she could be friendly and tended to regard most people with a positive attitude. She wasn't sure about some of the attendees at the party though and didn't care to see them again.

"They weren't all bad. I mean, nothing came up missing anyway," Evelyn remarked.

"I still don't understand why they were necessary. You didn't even know half of them. Seemed like a waste, especially for your summer party."

"I told you, they had their purpose. They were there was as a counterbalance, so Shannon could see what a jewel he has in Joya, comparatively speaking."

It made sense, Gail supposed, the part about comparisons. Because with Joya, there was none. But it all seemed like a waste of time and resources. Of course, if Shannon and Joya hit it off, then she had no complaints.

"And in any case, there's always my Independence Day cookout, so we're still good."

Gail shook her head. She recalled being anxious when she had to plan her and Earnest's annual Christmas party when they were younger. She couldn't imagine hosting as many get-togethers as Evelyn did.

"So, what about Joya? Did she say anything?" Evelyn continued.

Gail could hear Joya moving around in the kitchen and hushed her voice even more.

"Not a thing."

"What? Speak up. You know I'm old. I can't hear you."

Gail rolled her eyes.

"Nothing," she said a little louder. "She didn't say anything."

Gail had asked her general questions about the party, not wanting to arouse Joya's suspicions. Her daughter-in-law only responded in her usual chipper tone. Just friends, she said, in a rush of words that told her she really did believe that. But she and Shannon were in the kitchen for an hour talking and laughing. There had to be more.

"Well, that's fine. We're planting seeds. Getting them used to each other. You know that saying about familiarity…"

Gail thought about it for a moment.

"It breeds contempt?"

"No," Evelyn snapped, then thought about it herself. "I don't remember. Just be at church Sunday with Joya. Men look at the outside, how pretty a woman is, but for women, it's the inside that counts. And any man who has his priorities set—God first, his momma, then his family—there's nothing sexier to a woman. Joya will see that."

It seemed wrong to Gail to use the church as a location for their matchmaking, but since she didn't have any other ideas, she didn't argue. She simply told Evelyn, "I hope you know what you're doing."

"Trust me, okay?"

"Famous last words."

Evelyn said something else, but Gail didn't hear it because Joya was calling her.

"I gotta go," she said quickly and hung up her phone. Then she placed it on the dresser beside her and relaxed some, trying to look innocent. Or at least guiltless, which Gail learned from Evelyn was not the same thing.

Joya stuck her head inside the door.

"Hey."

"Oh, hey baby," Gail said, in her most surprised tone.

"I'm heading to work now," Joya said. "Did you need anything?"

"No, I'm alright," the older woman replied.

"Okay. Give me a call if you do."

Gail nodded and laid her head back as if she was getting ready to rest. When she heard Joya leave though, she got up and walked over to the window to watch her daughter-in-law pull out of the driveway. She would only be working half a day today, but it gave Gail a few precious hours to get done what she needed to do.

She shuffled to the bathroom and did her business. Then she walked over to her closet, turned the light on and retrieved the large picture box she kept in the shelf above. It wasn't heavy, but it still weighed heavy on her for different reasons. She didn't go into it very often for all the memories it carried. Today it was necessary.

Gail strode back to her bed with it and sat down. She placed the box in front her and carefully removed the lid. Inside were the mementoes she kept of Earnest, dating all the way back to when they first met. Earnest was the romantic type and not a day passed that he didn't express his love for her. Even when he was dying of cancer, he made sure she knew how much she meant to him. Which only made his passing that much more heartbreaking. No, she wasn't the only person to be devastated by the loss of a spouse, but God, it hurt to be left behind. Even now, years later, she still cried when she looked through the pictures.

Their wedding day …

Earnest's birthdays …

Gail's birthdays …

Their anniversaries …

The birth of their son, Michael …

His milestones …

His graduation from school and boot camp …

Earnest was gone by the time Michael became an officer and so he never got to see him in uniform, proudly serving his country. He never got to meet Joya, never got to love her as a daughter, never got to know about living abroad or starting life anew. He was gone by the time all of that happened, and though well-meaning family and friends tried to tell her he was still a part of her life, all she could feel was the void he left. She would see him one day again, she was sure of that; before that happened though, she needed to get things in order.

Gail carefully set the photos aside, and dug down a little deeper, searching for Earnest's old phone book. She had thought to get rid of it, inputting everything into her phone. But like everything else in the box, it was a part of Earnest. All the entries were written in his handwriting. Even the convenience of having names and numbers at the touch of her fingertips wasn't enough to give it up.

She scanned the pages until she came to the number she needed—that of Aaron Schell, Earnest's financial advisor. She picked her phone up off the dresser and dialed his number. She got his secretary and was able to make an appointment for that morning. Gail hung up, carefully replaced everything she had taken out and left the box on the dresser. Maybe she would look through it again later. Until then she had to get ready.

Eight

JOYA PARKED HER CAR IN THE corner spot of the church lot and walked back to the front where she left Gail. They normally went to the Baptist church Gail grew up in, but Evelyn had invited them to her church for their Friends and Family Day. Joya was looking forward to it. She enjoyed Evelyn's company; and admittedly, enjoyed spending time with Shannon as well. He was fast becoming a good friend.

Joya met Gail and they walked into the church together, where they were greeted by an usher. They joined Evelyn who was waiting for them inside the sanctuary.

"Oh, you made it," she said with a big smile on her face.

"Of course, we did," Joya replied as she hugged the woman. "We wouldn't miss it."

"Well you are sweet, aren't you?"

"That's what they keep telling me."

They sat down near the front and watched as the church started filling up. Joya sat on the other side of Gail who was seated beside her friend. While the two talked, Joya looked over the program. She recognized the fact that she was the third wheel in this relationship, but she didn't mind.

The service started and after a brief prayer, the choir stood up to sing. Joya was listening to the soulful melodies when someone took a seat beside her. She moved over, only to realize it was Shannon.

"Hey stranger," she whispered, leaning back towards him, so as not to disturb or distract those around them.

"What are you doing here?" he asked, smiling.

"Your mom invited us."

He nodded and sat back to listen to the choir. Joya did the same, but she liked that she was no longer the odd man out. She had never really thought about whether he went to church or not and was pleased to see that he wasn't just there. He paid attention, and when the pastor got up to speak, he actually opened his Bible and followed along. He wasn't vocal like Evelyn was, but he was present and that counted just as much.

Joya listened as well. She had been raised Catholic but opted to change denominations when she married Michael. It wasn't a difficult change—they all believed in the same God. It boiled down to the method of worship and truthfully, Joya appreciated the livelier services. She didn't fall asleep as often.

And now with that confession, I need to

repent, she thought.

Or at the very least, pay attention, like Shannon.

The smell of food began wafting through the church, causing Joya's stomach to growl. She turned her attention to the windows on her left, where she could see the tables that had been set up outside for the potluck lunch. Several parishioners were organizing the meal, while the pastor preached his sermon. Joya could see casseroles, breads, side dishes and desserts. Her stomach growled again. She should have eaten breakfast. Then she noticed she wasn't the only one watching the lunch scene unfold. Several women on the row in front of her were turning heads and commenting on the dishes. Joya tried to concentrate, but it was all so distracting. Thankfully, though, the pastor kept the sermon brief and ended it sooner than expected so that the congregation could fellowship.

Joya made a mental note of what she should confess for later, then stood up when the pastor closed the service with prayer. She followed Evelyn and Gail to the back of the sanctuary, where the pastor was talking to everyone as they exited. Shannon walked behind them.

"So how often do you guys do events like

this?" she asked, making small talk with Shannon.

"We try to do something every other month or so. Honestly, though, I miss as many days as I attend because of work."

Joya nodded understandingly as they inched up closer to the front of the line. Evelyn and Gail were deep in conversation and paid them no mind.

"So, have you decided what you're doing with your summer yet?" Shannon asked her.

"Not yet. I'm still weighing options, because, you know, there are so many…," she replied, a little cheeky. "I haven't ruled out a part-time job, still looking to volunteer or maybe tutor. No one likes homework over summer break, but it's good to keep on top of things. I don't know, really."

"And the only thing I don't hear you saying is that you're going to relax."

Joya smiled sheepishly.

"I guess I could do that. It's not really something I'm good at though."

"Don't feel bad. I'd like to think I would relax if I had the chance to do so, but I'd probably find a million other things to do," Shannon assured her with a touch to her arm. Joya smiled in response. "What do you like to do?" he asked.

She considered the question for a moment.

"I like to read. One of my co-workers hosts a book club and let me borrow a box of books she's read over the past year. I'll probably work my way through those."

"Hmm. I can't say I'm much of a reader. Unless it's work-related, I don't have much time for it."

"Really? I guess my brain just works differently, because I can't imagine not reading."

Shannon just shrugged his shoulders in response.

"So, if I wrote a tell-all, dishing about...let's say, the dark, visceral world of first-grade teachers, would you read that?" she teased.

He raised his eyebrow in interest.

"Maybe. What are we talking about here? Fight clubs? Black markets?" he replied, encouraging her along.

"We are battling for dibs to the playground," she deadpanned. "There are some steamy parts that take place in the teachers' lounge with the fifth-grade gym teacher, but those will be overshadowed by the quest our heroine embarks on as she searches for love and fulfillment. I'll title it The Book of Joy, because you know..."

She paused for dramatic effect and waited on him to fill-in the blank.

"Your name…?"

"Exactly."

He laughed, amused by her comments, but then conceded, "Okay yes, I would read that."

Joya smiled triumphantly. She turned around and saw Evelyn and Gail still talking. They had shuffled along further and were third in line to talk to the pastor.

"Do you write?" Shannon asked her.

Joya turned back to him.

"Lesson plans mostly," she replied honestly. "I used to write when I was younger. Short stories. But life happened."

"Have you thought about writing again?"

Joya shrugged her shoulders.

"Maybe. Call it corny, but I prefer to focus on writing my life rather than a story, you know what I mean?"

Shannon nodded understandingly.

"I get it," he said. The line moved, and they stepped forward with it. "So, what does Joya mean?" he asked. "I've not heard it before."

"It's Spanish for jewel. A family name," Joya responded quickly. She didn't like talking about her family. They asked her to make a difficult decision years ago and she made it, with no regrets. But that left her with just her name. Ultimately, she was okay with that. She'd find the joy in it, no pun intended this time.

Shannon simply smiled though.

"I like it. It fits you."

"As much as your name fits you?" she teased. She saw his eyes glaze over with embarrassment.

"You swore," he reminded her.

She smiled big and leaned her head back against his chest.

"I might have to renegotiate the terms. This one's too good to just swear to."

"Sounds like you'll need a lawyer for that."

"You know any?"

"I might. But they don't come cheap."

"Oh, I'm sure we can come to some agreement."

"You mean blackmail?"

"I prefer to call it a mutual understanding."

He stared at her, one eyebrow cocked.

"What do you want?" he asked.

"What are you willing to give me?"

"Whatsoever you desire. You tell me."

"Oh, a blank check. This could get interesting."

Their conversation died down as they realized they were next in line to see the pastor. Joya kept her attention forward as the couple in front of the four of them said their hellos to the cleric and moved on. An older, black man, he smiled when he saw Evelyn and greeted them all warmly. He shook Shannon's hand and offered the same to Joya. She liked his sincerity, but his acknowledgment of her left her self-conscious.

"You must be Joya," he said. "Evelyn has shared many good things about you, like how you moved with your mother-in-law here after the passing of your husband. Just like the Biblical Ruth. God will bless you for your actions."

He continued, but Joya only smiled politely. Indeed, she was very much aware of the similarities between her and the Biblical heroine, but she hated the comparisons.

Disliked. She disliked the comparison, she reminded herself.

Joya felt Shannon's hand on the small of her back and realized Evelyn and Gail had moved on. They caught up to the two and together, they joined the rest of the congregation outside. The older women found a table in the shade while Joya and Shannon got in the food line. Children ran past them, families fellowshipped together, and everyone seemed to be enjoying themselves.

After eating, Joya talked Shannon into participating in the potato sack race. They were unevenly paired and found it difficult to run together, but it was fun nonetheless. Several of the other men started a pickup game of basketball with Shannon and she was happy to cheer him on. In all that, Joya found she was actually relaxing.

They were there for a couple of hours before the crowds started thinning. Joya and Gail said their goodbyes and walked over to her car.

"Did you have fun?" Gail asked her as they got in.

"Yes. I really enjoyed it," Joya replied. She pulled out of the parking lot and turned in the direction of home.

"I'd say we all did. Shannon looked like he was having fun."

Joya nodded her agreement.

"You two were busy chatting away."

"He's easy to talk to," she said, then quickly added, "Like Evelyn."

"It was good seeing you smiling and laughing again. You looked good together."

Joya detected no insinuations in her tone. Still she felt the need to expound.

"He's a friend, that's all. A good friend."

Nine

THE DOORBELL RANG.

"I got it," Hannah announced, jumping off the chair she was standing on in the kitchen.

Evelyn quickly grabbed her arm and said, "Hold on, Missy. Remember, we don't just answer the door to anyone."

Ashley had called her that morning and apologetically asked if Evelyn could watch Hannah for the day. Evelyn quickly assented, as she didn't have anything else on her agenda. However, she soon discovered the little girl had a boundless amount of energy, where hers was limited. After eating a snack, Hannah decided she wanted to play beauty salon. Using her own collection of make-up, which consisted of several flavored lip glosses, a blush palette and three tubes of scented lotions, the little girl proceeded to work on Evelyn. She applied all her glosses to the old woman's lips, all the blush to her face then lubed up her arms and face. She was working on Evelyn's hair when the doorbell rang. The woman stood up and together, they walked to the living room to answer the door. Evelyn caught a glimpse of herself in the mirror above her mantle. Her lips were done up three times bigger their normal size. Several, uneven layers of blush covered her face; and her hair was combed out into a wild afro. She was a sight to behold and hoped no one important was at the door.

It was only Gail though—a different kind of important.

Her friend's eyes went wide as she took in Evelyn's face and hair. Neither had a chance to greet the other though. Realizing she had a new customer, Hannah released Evelyn's hand, took Gail's and pulled her into the house.

"Welcome to Hannah's beauty salon," she exclaimed. "My name is Hannah."

"Well, hello Hannah," Gail played along. "My name is Gail."

"You're just in time. I'm done with Ms. Evelyn. It's your turn."

Gail's mouth opened to object, but Hannah was already detailing her planned beauty treatment for the woman. Evelyn was happy to get a break for a few minutes. She shut the door and followed them into the kitchen.

"I think I might pass," Gail said, with a little apprehension, as she took a seat at the table.

Evelyn was not going to let her get away that easy though.

"Oh, no. Hannah, make Ms. Gail beautiful. Just like you made me."

Hannah jumped up and down with anticipation.

Gail didn't argue, but she did give Evelyn a look that told her exactly how she really felt about the make-over. And it was not good.

While Evelyn fixed them both a cup of tea, Hannah started on Gail. Her hair was shorter, but that didn't stop the little girl from combing it out and dressing it up with barrettes and twists.

"You're doing good, Hannah girl," Evelyn encouraged her.

The little girl beamed from the compliment, while Gail pursed her lips in annoyance. Evelyn knew this wasn't what the older woman signed up for when she decided to visit, but as her friend, she was only too happy to share the joy. And it was joy, pure and simple. Seeing Hannah enjoying herself, discovering new things, playing in her new surroundings—it was all bliss. Granted, Evelyn could barely keep up with the child, but she enjoyed watching her and encouraging her nonetheless. And if Jackie would ever decide to get off his ass and declare his love to Joya, then Evelyn could do the same with her own granddaughter one day. How fortuitous that day would be.

"Now, it's time for make-up," Hannah announced.

Gail groaned.

Evelyn decided to grant the woman some pity.

"Hannah, baby, let's give Ms. Gail a moment to get ready, okay?"

"Huh?" the girl uttered in disappointment.

"Let Ms. Gail rest before you do her make-up, okay?"

Hannah's countenance dropped, tugging at Evelyn's heart strings.

"'Tell you what, go upstairs to my room and get the rest of my make-up."

The little girl brightened up and ran upstairs.

"You just gave her run of the house, huh?" Gail said, relaxing into her chair. She picked up the hand mirror that was on the table with the rest of Hannah's beauty products and grimaced at her reflection.

"Oh stop, you look fine. Hannah's just the creative sort," Evelyn stated, as she handed Gail a cup of tea. She changed the subject. "So, did Joya say anything about Sunday?"

Gail shook her head.

"They're friends, that's all."

"She didn't tell him that, did she?"

A comment like that was usually the kiss

of death for any relationship looking to move from the platonic stage.

"I don't know. I mean they seemed like they were having a good time. Maybe they really are just friends."

Evelyn sat next to Gail and sighed. She hadn't even considered that outcome. She was already struggling with the possibility that her son might never get married. She had always joked around that he was the particular sort, but she wasn't entirely sure there wasn't more there. She and Jack had raised him to be independent, like her, but he seemed to be more like his father, quiet and content. Maybe he really was satisfied being on his own.

Evelyn shook her head.

"I don't believe that. You saw them. There's something there."

"Well, you and I see it, but apparently, they don't. So, what do we do?"

"Listen, it's only been a couple of weeks," Evelyn advised. "They just need to spend more time together. We ain't giving up yet."

Hannah came running back into the kitchen at that moment, a large make-up case in her hands.

"Look what I found," she said, enthralled with her new treasure. She deposited the case on the table and jumped up on the chair to inspect its contents. She pulled everything out of the case and arranged it on the table according to type and color. She set the pencils beside each other, the lipsticks next to them, followed by the blush and the eye shadow. She also found some nail polish and glitter. Whether she wanted to or not, Gail was going to look fabulous.

"We're ready!" Hannah announced with an expectancy that could hardly be contained.

Gail sighed with resignation. "Alright child, go ahead and finish my make-over."

Hannah smiled and went to work on her face. Evelyn watched for a little while, before deciding to complete some chores, now that Hannah was distracted. She finished her tea and washed the dishes. Then she remembered she had started a load of laundry earlier that morning. She went to the basement door and turned on the lights. It was still under lit, but she knew where every crack, every dent, every step was. She had taken them a million times over the last five decades. Even still, she was a few stairs shy of the bottom when she somehow missed a step. It caught her by surprise and caused her to tumble down the remaining stairs. She landed hard at the bottom.

Ten

GAIL SAT IN THE WAITING ROOM of the hospital watching Hannah, who was surprisingly well-purported, given the situation. Evelyn had broken her wrist and sprained her ankle. They had to call for an ambulance. While the paramedics helped Evelyn onto the stretcher, Gail cleaned up her face and got ready to follow. She called Ashley, who promised to meet them at the hospital.

Now waiting, Gail was starting to get anxious, but she forced herself to remain calm for Hannah's sake. It seemed the little girl was comfortable where she was though. She sat on the edge of her seat, staring at the doorway to the waiting room as if waiting for someone.

A young nurse walked by and greeted the little girl.

"Hi Hannah," she said.

Hannah waved back. The nurse continued walking.

Gail thought the nurse might be a family friend. Then a doctor walked by and greeted the little girl in the same fashion.

"Do you know who that was?" she asked the child.

Hannah shrugged her shoulders and turned back to the doorway. Eventually, she got up the nerve to go investigate. Gail didn't stop her, but watched as Hannah moved closer, leaning on one of the chairs as she stuck her head out of the door. Gail worried for a moment that she might run off, but Hannah didn't seem to want to venture out any further. She simply sat and waited.

A third hospital staff member walked by and waved at Hannah. She smiled and waved back. Gail was ready to enquire when a young woman rushed in.

"Hannah!"

"Mommy!" the little girl exclaimed and ran into her mother's arms.

Gail collected herself and walked over to the pair.

"How's Ms. Evelyn?" Ashley asked, setting her daughter down.

"They're still looking at her."

"I'll wait with you, if you don't mind."

Gail nodded her head and sat in the closest chair. Ashley joined her, but Hannah resumed her position at the door. Gail continued watching her, even as her mother made light conversation. After a few minutes, another doctor walked by and waved at Hannah. Ashley must have seen the confusion on Gail's face, because she explained, "We spent a lot of time in the hospital when Hannah was younger."

"Oh, was she sick?"

Ashley shook her head, her expression sheepish.

"No, just a magnet for trouble. She was always doing something that landed us in the emergency room: stuck a rock up her nose once, ate crayons and baby wipes regularly, jumped off high places and fractured limbs. She bruised her sternum once and managed to break her coccyx another time. We've gotten to know the hospital staff really well. She's mellowed out since then, but I think she misses them sometimes."

Gail smiled.

"I think they miss her too."

Ashley guffawed.

"No offense meant, but *I* don't miss any of them," she said.

The two women continued talking, until Joya rushed in, the same worried expression on her face that Ashley bore earlier. Gail assured her Evelyn would be alright, then introduced her to Ashley and Hannah. After a while, Shannon joined them. The five of them waited to get news on Evelyn. Well, the adults did. Hannah continued her vigil at the door, as if waiting for one particular person. Eventually that person did walk by—a tall, dark-haired man in scrubs. Hannah smiled big and ran to him.

"Dr. Tory," she exclaimed, and offered him a hug.

He returned the sentiment, happy to see her. He picked her up and walked her back to her mother. Again, Ashley's expression bordered on embarrassment.

"Hannah's pediatrician," she clarified and stood to her feet. They exchanged pleasantries, before he asked, "What's going on?"

Ashley explained what happened with Evelyn. The doctor placed Hannah on her feet.

"I'll see if I can get you some news."

"Thank you, Dr. Jamison."

"Anything for my favorite patient," he said, with a wink to Hannah. He nodded to their group and left the room to see if he could get information on Evelyn. Gail was sure she was being taken care of but given Evelyn's advanced age, there was much that could go wrong if it wasn't discovered in time. Gail understood that better than anyone else.

Dr. Jamison returned in minutes.

"They're setting the cast now. You should be able to see her shortly."

"Thank you, doctor," Shannon said, his

concern audible.

"You're welcome. And good luck," he said, before leaving them.

Hannah was more relaxed now that she had seen the person she had her heart set on seeing and she returned to her usual antics. She was a little more active, more curious and ready to get in trouble, when Evelyn's doctor finally came out to see them. The older woman would need to stay off her feet while her leg healed, but she would recover just fine. As a precaution, they wanted her to stay in the hospital overnight to monitor her.

Even though only family members were allowed to visit, the doctor permitted all of them to go see her. Joya put her arm around Gail as they walked to Evelyn's room.

"Are you alright?" she asked her, slowing down her pace to keep up with the older woman.

"I'm not the one who got hurt."

"No, but she's your friend and what hurts one, hurts us all."

"I'm fine. Don't worry about me."

"I know, but I couldn't even imagine what I would do if that was you. I'm just grateful you were there."

Gail nodded, but she didn't say anything else.

"Here we are," the doctor advised as she

stopped in front of Evelyn's room. "Let me know if you need anything."

The group entered the room quietly, expecting the older woman to be resting after such a traumatic experience. But no, she was sitting up in her bed, her right arm in a cast, her right leg propped up on a pillow, fighting with a male nurse who was trying to take her blood pressure.

"I told you I'm fine," she insisted, throwing the cuff at him. She noticed her guests and turned to her son for defense. "Will you tell him I'm fine?"

Shannon stepped up, a heavy sigh on his breath.

"Ma, what are you doing?"

"I'm tired of being poked and prodded. I want to go home," she exclaimed.

Gail shook her head and found a chair. Why she worried, she didn't know. Evelyn was invincible.

The nurse quit trying to check her blood pressure and advised he would be back later. Everyone else gathered around the bed. Ashley stopped Hannah from climbing up, but Evelyn gave her permission to do so. The little girl was well-behaved, but seemed fascinated with Evelyn's cast, which in turn caused her mother to worry that she might want one of her own. Ashley cut the visit short but promised to come over the next day to help her. She picked up her daughter and said good-bye to everyone. Once they were gone, the atmosphere changed.

"I know you don't want to hear this, but we need to talk about that house," Shannon began, using more force in his tone than Gail thought was called for. But knowing her friend the way she did, this was probably a conversation Evelyn and Shannon had had in the past and Evelyn had probably refused to entertain. Force was necessary.

"I am just fine, thank you for asking," Evelyn replied, indignantly.

"You're not fine. Look at you."

"It was an accident. They happen you know."

Shannon sighed.

"I want for you to come live with me."

Evelyn frowned.

"I'm not moving."

"Well, you can't stay by yourself."

"I'm not senile."

"No, but you're not a young woman anymore, no matter what you feel."

Evelyn pursed her lips, angrily.

"Your father built that house for me. He built it for *us*. I'm. Not. Moving. You want me out of there? You'll have to drag my cold corpse out of it!"

"This is ridiculous," Shannon exclaimed. "That house is too much for you. You're always complaining about it."

"That doesn't mean I want to move," she returned. "Why don't you just move in with me?"

"I am not moving back home."

"How is that any different than me staying with you?"

"It's different."

"Look who's being ridiculous now."

"Ma, listen to yourself…"

Shannon was beyond frustrated and struggled to find the right words. Gail opened her mouth to help him, when Joya stepped up and touched his arm to draw his attention towards her. She wore a sympathetic expression on her face that begged for his permission to get involved. He threw his hands up in resignation, dismissed the argument already on his tongue and turned away as Joya tagged in and took over the conversation.

"We're just worried about you, Ms. Evelyn. Imagine if Gail hadn't been there. This could have been much worse. We love you and want what's best for you."

Gail couldn't believe her eyes.

"Listen to her," Shannon insisted as he turned back to his mother. "Obviously you're not listening to me."

"I know how much you love that house," Joya continued, "but we need *you* more than we need *it*."

Gail watched with astonishment as the two went back and forth, speaking in one accord, and with one purpose. How did they not see it? How could they allege they were only friends when there was obviously more there? Gail had her doubts before, but not anymore.

"Great. Now he's turned you against me? You want to chime in Gail?" Evelyn contended.

Gail stood up and walked over to her friend's bedside. She needed her friend to stop arguing so she could see what was happening between Shannon and Joya.

"Actually—"

Evelyn let out an exasperated breath and threw up her good hand.

"I can't believe this…"

Gail nudged her side trying to maintain a certain amount of subtlety so as not to be noticed by Shannon and Joya. Evelyn continued ranting though.

"I am not moving…"

Gail hit her friend harder, but it didn't seem to make a difference.

"And that's it…"

She gave it one last try. She hit Evelyn in her side with the back of her hand. Evelyn cried out.

"Ow! What is wrong with you?"

Gail smiled and moved her eyes towards Shannon and Joya. The woman, however, seemed oblivious to everything around her and only frowned at her. Gail decided to try a different approach. She straightened up and met Shannon's gaze. Both he and Joya were glaring at her in confusion, trying to figure out what was going on between her and Evelyn.

"Maybe we should talk about it later," Gail suggested innocently. "I mean, if she has to spend the night, there's no harm in postponing the conversation, right?"

Shannon sighed and agreed.

"We are talking about it though."

Evelyn started to argue, but Gail pinched the closest pound of flesh to her hand. She saw Evelyn grimace, but the woman didn't say anything. She changed the subject, but Shannon and Evelyn were so stressed out at this point, she and Joya were the only ones talking. Fortunately, an office administrator walked in, asking to speak with the financially responsible party. Happy for the distraction, Shannon introduced himself and agreed to help her fill out the necessary paperwork.

Gail interrupted.

"I grabbed your mom's purse, but left it in the car," she told him, then turned to Joya. "Maybe you can go get it," she suggested, knowing Shannon was too much of a gentleman to allow her to run this errand. She was right.

"I'll get it," he volunteered.

Joya smiled her appreciation, then turned to the administrator and told her she would help her until he returned. Gail gave Shannon her keys and advised him where she was parked. After the three of them left, Evelyn demanded, "What the hell was that about?" She was still glowering at Gail.

"Weren't you listening?" Gail asked.

"Yes, they want me to sell the house—"

"Exactly. *They*—"

"Yes, they want me to move and—"

Gail rolled her eyes. It seemed the fall had made her friend slightly denser.

"*They*," she said again. "It wasn't just Shannon or Joya making the case, it was *both of them*. They were acting as one. You got it now?"

Understanding seemed to dawn on Evelyn's face, but she fought it with every breath in her body.

"I'm not selling my house."

"Do you want a house? Or do you want a daughter-in-law?"

Evelyn avoided her gaze, angrily breathing through her nostrils.

"You saw them," Gail continued. "There's something there and if we don't help them, they're not going to see it. You said it yourself, they just need to spend time together. This could be the opportunity for them to do that. Let Shannon clean the house some, fix it up, whatever. Joya will jump at the chance to help and while they're doing that, they'll see what we do. So just agree to it, okay? Tell them…I don't know. Whatever would make Shannon believe you had a change of heart and give them this chance to find love."

Evelyn still looked unconvinced.

"Just play along for a while," Gail pleaded. "Isn't that what you would say?"

"If it was your house, sure," she returned bitterly. "But what happens if this doesn't work? I'm out of a daughter-in-law and a house."

"We won't let it go that far, okay? What do you say, Evelyn?"

The woman pouted. Frowned. Bit the inside of her cheek. But she didn't argue.

Eleven

SHANNON OPENED THE DOOR TO his car and helped his mother out. She struggled to walk on her bad ankle and though he had gotten her a crutch, she couldn't use it because her arm was in a cast. The only upside to all this was that Evelyn wasn't going anywhere. Unfortunately, this meant she would need assistance with her every day errands. He had requested a couple of weeks off of work to help her, but beyond that, he wasn't sure how everything was going to play out. Evelyn had yet to talk to him about the house and knowing his mother, Shannon was certain there was no way she was going to agree to move. Even with this being in her best interest, she would fight him tooth and nail.

He walked with her to the side door, where Hannah stood waiting for them. Behind her were Joya and Ashley. Shannon was touched by their concern for his mother, especially Joya. The woman stood with him when it came to what was best for Ms. Evelyn; and not just that, she calmly took charge of the conversation when he got flustered. Whatever argument he had about not pursuing Joya was suddenly moot in his mind.

"Welcome home," Hannah announced with a wide grin. She stepped back away from the door to give Evelyn space to enter, pushing her mother and Joya along with her. Shannon was amused by her actions, as was Evelyn, who smiled and patted the little girl's head.

"Well, thank you," Evelyn replied, her breathing labored. She stopped long enough to catch her breath, then continued onto the living room and over to the couch where she sat back. Hannah joined her as Shannon pulled up an ottoman and helped her get comfortable.

"Are you okay?" he asked her.

She waved him off, annoyed with all the attention she was getting.

"I'm fine. Just get me the remote."

"I'll get it," Hannah volunteered. She got up and ran to the television where it was located. She returned with the remote and the two started channel surfing, ignoring Shannon as he hovered over them. Accepting that he was his mother's least favorite person right now, Shannon said, "I'll make you some tea," and exited the room. He walked into the kitchen where Ashley and Joya were busy talking and fixing lunch.

"Where's Gail?" he asked Joya as he pulled out the tea kettle and filled it up with water.

"She wasn't feeling well this morning," Joya responded. "She's resting."

She didn't sound concerned about her mother-in-law, so Shannon didn't worry. God only knew he had enough to worry about with his mother. He didn't need or want to have to be anxious about his auntie as well.

Shannon set the kettle on the stove and turned to Ashley.

"Thanks for doing all this," he told her.

"I'm happy to help in any way I can," she said. She wiped her hand on a towel and added, "I should go check on Hannah, make sure she's not bugging her."

"They're getting along just great. You don't have to worry," Shannon assured her.

Ashley smiled appreciatively but excused herself anyway. He took a seat at the table and tried to relax for a moment. He was distracted by Joya though as she found a mug, unwrapped the tea bag and waited for the water to boil.

"Did you get a chance to talk to her on the way home?" she asked him.

"No," he said, curious at the way she was working *with* him without being asked. "No, she wouldn't hear it. She's stubbornly attached to the house."

"Well, your dad did build it for her."

"I know. But in the end, it's just a house.

It's the people around you who make a house a home."

"While that's true," Joya said, cautiously, dropping into the seat next to him, "You have to see it from her perspective. She's got you, but you also have a lot going on."

And that was the crux of the matter, the thing Evelyn kept coming back to: it was him and only him. He had given her no daughter-in-law, no children. There were no family Christmases, no family dinners or no significant events that other families experienced. It was him and just him.

Joya touched his arm, drawing him out of his thoughts.

"I didn't mean to guilt you. She's got a lot of connections to this house, a lot of memories. And right now, she's just lonely, that's all. Maybe this will help her—having everyone around her, showing her where her home truly is."

Shannon glared at Joya as she spoke. He didn't mean to, but he couldn't help it. She had a way of looking at a situation and seeing the positive in it that he had seen in few people. She wasn't just beautiful on the outside, but also on the inside. She was as her name implied—a jewel. A rare one.

"You're right," he finally told her. "But I can't change the situation. Just make sure she's safe."

"And you're a good son for it. She'll see that," Joya assured him.

"Knock, knock," a familiar voice interrupted them. Shannon turned around to see Nathan at the door with flowers in his hand. Shannon told him about his mother when he requested time off, but he didn't expect the man to show up at her house. That was Nathan though—a good boss and a good friend.

"Hey," Shannon said. He stood up and shook his hand. "What are you doing here?"

"Checking in on your mom," he replied. Shannon introduced him to Joya, then showed him to the living room where Evelyn and Hannah were sitting on the couch watching one of her soap operas.

"There's my favorite septuagenarian," Nathan said in a flirty tone.

Evelyn sat up and smiled at him as he handed her the flowers and kissed her on the cheek.

"Oh Nathan! Thank you so much," she gushed. She turned the bouquet over in her hand and smelled the flowers.

"They're pretty," Hannah said.

"Yes, they are," Evelyn agreed.

Ashley offered to put them in water. Evelyn handed them to her, and she and her daughter left the room. Nathan dropped into the now vacant seat beside her.

"How're you doing, Evelyn?"

"I'm fine. It was just an accident."

"And accidents do happen," he agreed.

"You need to tell Jackie that, because he wants me to move now."

Shannon started to argue, but Nathan kept talking as if he wasn't even there.

"Well, you can just move in with me," he said, with a wink of the eye.

Evelyn raised an eyebrow.

"Oh, honey, I don't think you could handle all this," she said.

"Come on. Obviously, I'm your type."

"Oh, and what is that?"

"The vanilla to your chocolate," he replied in a slow, sultry voice. He took her hand in his and kissed it.

Evelyn laughed.

Shannon gagged.

"Look, I know I can't compete with Jack," Nathan said, "But this white man has skills too. What do you say?"

"You're too young for me, baby," she said, her tone playful.

"That just means I've got the stamina to keep up."

Shannon had heard enough. He turned around and left the room. They had innocently flirted in the past to a small degree, but this was too much. It was disgusting to watch, disgusting to think about. Shannon walked by Joya, who standing at the doorway, watching and smiling. She followed him back to the kitchen.

"That was funny," she said.

"No, it wasn't," he insisted.

"Oh, come on. They were just having a little fun."

Shannon shook his head, unwilling not only to accept it, but to hear it as well.

Nathan visited for a few more minutes before backtracking into the kitchen to say goodbye.

"Reece, your mom is great. I should bring her along on my next speed date. She'd kill it."

Shannon winced.

"Why do you do that? She's an elderly woman."

"No, she's a badass woman, who can give it as good as she takes it," Nathan said, admiringly. "Gives me something to aspire to."

"Yeah, there's a name for that—creepy, old guy."

Nathan smiled knowingly, as if he had achieved the very thing he had come to do—annoy Shannon. He got serious though and said, "Listen, take as much time as you need,

Reece. Just give me a call sometime this week about the thing. I need to get your client list."

Shannon shook his hand, appreciatively.

"I will. Thanks again."

He walked him out to his car, then returned to the kitchen, where Joya stood waiting for him.

"So, what's this *thing*?" she asked.

"It's nothing," he said, dismissively. Then added, "I made partner at the firm. We're hosting an open house mid-summer to officially announce it." Shannon treated it as par for course for his career of choice and while he didn't take for granted the blessings he had been given, he also didn't want anyone making a big deal out of it.

Anyone, except Joya, it seemed. He could feign ignorance and say he didn't know why he told her, but the truth was, he knew she would be happy for him and proud of his accomplishments. And he wanted that.

As expected, Joya smiled big, threw her arms around his neck and hugged him.

"Congratulations," she exclaimed, then released him. "That's wonderful."

"Thanks," he said, almost sheepishly.

"We should celebrate."

"Now's probably not a good time for it."

"Now is probably the best time for it. But I'll give you a pass this time."

He wasn't sure he wanted her to, but he nodded anyway, then went to check on his mother.

JOYA BUSIED herself washing the dishes, as Shannon left, and Ashley came back in. She could hear Hannah in the other room, talking to Evelyn as if they were contemporaries.

"I can't believe the way she's taken to Ms. Evelyn," Ashley remarked. "Hannah will talk to anyone, but ever since the bus incident, Evelyn's all she talks about."

"Well, the feeling is mutual. Evelyn is just enraptured with Hannah. We all are."

Ashley smiled and got back to what she was doing before she went to check on her daughter. They were preparing meals for the week, so Evelyn wouldn't have to cook.

"Do you and your husband live near here?" Ashley asked as she chopped up some onions for the casserole they were working on. Joya was so focused on her part of the recipe, she didn't immediately realize Ashley was talking to her. Then it was another minute before Joya understood Ashley was referring to Shannon.

"Oh, no, we're not married," she corrected her. "I'm just a family friend."

"I'm sorry. I assumed by the way you two were…" —she paused, seemingly searching for the right words. Joya was suddenly curious. She stopped what she was doing and turned to the young woman, causing her to blush— "…*friendly* with each other, I thought maybe you were married. Or together at least. You definitely make a cute couple."

Joya considered her actions around Shannon. Yes, she was friendly, but not any more so with him than with any one else…right?

You did just hug him.

I would have hugged anyone else with the same news.

Would she have though? Joy wasn't so sure now. So, what made Shannon any different?

The way he gets you… the way he listens to you… the way he looks at you…

Or maybe you just miss Michael so much you're projecting what you want onto Shannon.

Joya wasn't sure of anything anymore. She and Shannon were friends, she knew that. They shared a common experience, caring for older family members. They appreciated each other. But there was nothing more and she wasn't sure there could ever be, not when she was already in love with her husband. He might have been gone, but it didn't change the way she felt about him. Joya didn't begrudge anyone who remarried after losing a spouse. She just wasn't sure it was in her to do it.

"No," she finally said, as the tea kettle started whistling. "We're just friends."

Joya turned the burner off, quickly made the tea, then left for the living room.

"I've got fifty years of life here," Evelyn was saying. "Fifty years of memories. Are you seriously asking me to give that up?"

"No, Ma—"

"It's not something I can just throw into a box and move somewhere else," she snapped at Shannon. When she saw Joya, her countenance changed. She accepted the cup with a smile and in a lighter tone, said, "Thank you, sweetheart."

"Of course," Joya responded. "Did you need anything else?"

"This is enough for now."

The younger woman decided to hang around rather than return to the kitchen. She moved towards the side of the couch, where Shannon was sitting. She considered for a moment how her choice of where to stand might look like she was trying to be close to Shannon, but Hannah was seated on the other side of Evelyn and if Joya tried to sit anywhere else, she would likely draw more attention to herself than she wanted. Joya was flustered for a second. She was never the type to let what others thought of her dictate how she acted. Deciding she wasn't going to start now, Joya determined to stay where she was. And to continue being 'friendly' with Shannon, if that's what the situation called for.

"Ma, you're a pack rat," Shannon said. "When was the last time you were in the attic?"

"I don't know. But it doesn't matter. All those things are important to me."

"And the basement?"

"I was in there yesterday. Did you forget?" she asked, her tone heavy with sarcasm. She raised her casted arm as evidence.

"And all that stuff downstairs?"

Evelyn was defiantly quiet.

"Look, I get it," Shannon said, softening his tone. "Your life is here. But I need you safe. Please, Ma."

Evelyn eyed him with equal parts malice and understanding. Joya could see he had won part of her, but she wasn't going down without a fight. Instead she sighed angrily and stated, "I want a party."

"You just had one," he declared.

"For Independence Day. I have an annual get-together with the family to celebrate the birth of this fine nation. You're asking me to give up my life as I know it. Well, the least you can do is give me that."

"Ma, you're moving, not dying."

"That's what I want."

Shannon sighed. Without thinking, Joya squeezed his shoulder to encourage him. He glanced at her appreciatively before muttering, "Fine."

"I'm not moving out before then," Evelyn insisted.

"Fine."

"And I want a say in what gets thrown out."

Shannon looked like he was ready to argue. The work was harrowing as it was. If he had to go through her to clean up, he would never get done. Joya jumped into the conversation.

"I can help. I've got the summer off," she said, looking from Evelyn to Shannon. He glared at her dubiously, as if asking her if she really wanted to do that. But she did. She was happy to share the chore with him. "Really. I'd love to help."

Evelyn smiled and said, "Alright then."

Twelve

GAIL WATCHED JOYA LEAVE FOR Evelyn's house the next morning, then rushed to get ready. Well, rushed as much as she could. Even with a day of rest, Gail wasn't up to her usual strength. She felt discomfort in her limbs and in her bones.

It's all part of life, she told herself.

She had met with Aaron Schell earlier, but that meeting was about introductions. Now that they had been reacquainted and up-to-speed on what she needed from him, a follow-up appointment had been scheduled to finalize the changes to her will and estate. Unfortunately, the only time she could get with him was this morning. She didn't want to tell Joya where she was going because it would only upset her, but she didn't want to lie to Joya either, so she waited until the younger woman left to get ready. Only then did Gail shower up and get dressed. She thought about doing her hair. She was normally quite meticulous about her looks while out in public, but today she would have to settle for looking presentable. She grabbed a hat and left for her appointment.

Gail had all but ignored her finances after

Earnest passed. He had been the one who took care of paying the bills and saving towards their retirement. Even after his death though, he was still taking care of her. His retirement and life insurance policies helped her cover expenses, but this mode of existence wasn't good enough anymore. She needed to make sure everything was in order for Joya, much as Earnest did for her.

Gail arrived with a few minutes to spare. She parked her car in the adjacent garage and walked to the front door. After arriving on the appropriate floor, she announced herself to the receptionist, who showed her to a small conference room.

"Mr. Schell is finishing up a call, then he'll be right in," the woman informed her, before leaving.

Gail looked around and picked the closest seat to the door to wait. The room was sparsely furnished: there was a table with several chairs, a credenza with bottles of water on it and a television on the opposite wall. The environment itself was sterile and uninviting, but Gail supposed she wasn't there to feel at home. Not in her financial advisor's office and not especially with her reasons for visiting. Still, the sooner she was done, the better.

A few minutes passed. The temperature

in the room dropped. Gail had brought a sweater with her, but it didn't seem to be enough to drive the chill away. She got up and moved to the window, where the sun was shining through. They were on the ninth floor, giving her a wide view of the street below. There wasn't much to see though. The rooftop to the building beside them. The few people walking around below. An ice cream cart vendor. A homeless man lying down on a city bench.

Where was Aaron?

Gail grew more restless with every passing second. She was tired, her muscles were aching, and she wished she was home in bed. She should have done this another day. She should have told Joya and let her help. She should have...

Aaron, a white gentleman in his sixties, burst through the door with a stack of papers in his hand.

"Mrs. Evans, so glad to see you," he said. "Sorry I'm running late. I was on a phone call with one of my other clients."

"Okay, well I'm your client too," she said testily.

He smiled at her, a pitiful glance on his face.

"Yes, you are. And again, I'm sorry. Time sometimes just slips away from us."

His calm tone was chastising. Gail took a deep breath and settled down. So what if he was a few minutes late. It wasn't the worst thing in the world.

"You're right, it does. Forgive my curtness."

"No harm done, Mrs. Evans. Now since I've kept you waiting long enough…," he began, then dove into their meeting. He reviewed her and Earnest's portfolio of investments, delving into details that had no meaning for her. All she needed was the bottom line. Still Gail listened patiently. "Earnest was always conservative with his investments, but even those were money-makers. When you count all the stocks, investments and policies, your net worth is three point two million."

Aaron looked up at her for a reaction, but Gail wasn't surprised to hear the number. Like he said, Earnest was good with money and made sure his family was taken care of.

"Now, Earnest's will left everything to you and Michael," Aaron continued, "But I understand your son passed away last year?"

"That is correct."

There was little emotion in her voice—Michael's death was fact now.

"And he had no children."

"No. Just a wife."

Aaron looked down at the paper in front of him.

"Joy Evans?"

"Joy-*a* Evans."

Aaron picked up a pen and corrected the name on the sheet.

"And you want to leave everything to her."

"Correct. I want my will updated to reflect that and a no-resuscitation."

Aaron looked at her curiously, as if he wanted to question her decision. He didn't though.

"Is Joya aware of this change?" he asked instead.

"No. And she doesn't need to know. Not yet anyway."

Aaron put his pen down and glared at her solemnly.

"Is everything alright with you?" he asked with genuine concern.

"I'm old, Aaron," Gail said quickly. "That's all."

A cough tickled her throat. She covered her mouth and let it out. This only seemed to aggravate it. She covered her mouth and coughed until she couldn't anymore, then she sat back, almost embarrassed. Aaron got up and grabbed a bottle of water for her. He cracked open the lid and offered it to her. Gail started to take the bottle but noticed blood in her hand. She quickly dropped it onto her lap and reached out with her other hand. Then she took a sip and let it settle her throat.

"Are you okay?" he finally asked.

Gail nodded and said, her voice hoarse, "Just haven't been feeling well lately."

"Can I get you anything else?"

"No. I'm fine really."

He didn't appear to believe her, but he didn't argue either. Instead, he rose to his feet and let her know his secretary would update everything. Once he was gone, Gail cleaned her hand up with a tissue she had in her purse; then she waited patiently as everything was prepared for her signature. She reviewed the changes and signed where necessary. Documents were notarized; and within the hour, her will had been updated. With this task complete, Gail left the office and started her drive home. She felt like a burden had been lifted. She could die in peace now…or she could if Shannon and Joya would stop playing around and declare their love to one another.

Thirteen

SHANNON GOT UP BEFORE HIS alarm went off and sat at the edge of his bed.

No, *his* bed was at his apartment, on the other side of town. He was staying with his mother for the time being and had slept on the old twin-size bed in the spare bedroom. It was more springs than mattress and squeaked every time he turned around. He wasn't sure how much sleep he had actually gotten, but he was certain of one thing: when he started cleaning out his mother's house, this mattress would be the first thing to go.

Which reminded him: Joya was coming over today to help clean. Excited about the prospect of seeing her, Shannon got up and got ready for the day. He showered and shaved, then found a clean set of workout clothes. There was no logic in his actions since he would be getting dirty while working on the house, but he couldn't very well throw on some old sweats. He had to look presentable for Joya.

Evelyn was already up when he went downstairs. She had moved her bedroom to the ground floor years ago, so they didn't have to make too many modifications for her.

And apart from her current disability, she was adjusting well. *A little too well,* Shannon thought. He didn't expect her to give into his argument as quickly as she did, but he wasn't going to look a gift horse in the mouth. The fact that she agreed to move was big and he was going to keep the momentum going.

"Good morning, Ma," he said, as he kissed her on the forehead. She was seated at the kitchen table, her leg propped up on a chair, her casted arm resting on the table. She appeared no worse for wear, but still he cringed when he saw the dark coloration on her calf.

"Good morning, baby," she said.

"How'd you sleep?" he asked her, as he reached for a mug and poured himself some coffee.

"Alright. Hard to get comfortable with this cast."

"It'll get better."

"Where are you going?" she asked him. "I thought you were going to work on the house today."

"I am."

"Then why'd you shower?"

Because I am hopelessly infatuated and want to make a good impression on Joya.

"I…uhm, have to run to the store first."

She nodded but didn't comment anymore

on his appearance. He was grateful, because he didn't like lying to his mother. Not that it was a complete lie. She already had most of the items he needed to begin repairs, but there were a few things he would eventually need. Since he was dressed, it made sense for him to go ahead and make good on his lie. It was wrong, but if he didn't, his mother would call him out on it and this was the last thing he wanted.

"I made breakfast," she said, pointing to the stove.

Shannon shook his head.

"This will work for me, thanks," he responded, holding up his coffee. "Are you okay until I come back?"

She appeared amused by the question.

"I can function without you, you know."

Shannon smirked.

"Superwoman, are you?"

"In the flesh. Now go. I'll be fine."

He grabbed his wallet and keys and left for the home improvement store. By the time Shannon returned to the house, Joya had arrived. She was dressed in a simple pair of yoga pants and a feminine t-shirt, looking every bit of sexy as if she had worn a form-fitting evening gown that enhanced every one of her curves. She was seated at the table with Evelyn, eating breakfast and talking. When she saw him walk in, she smiled brightly, as if happy to see him.

If only that was the reaction he could come home to everyday…

"Good morning! Your mom was just telling me about the time you broke your arm."

Shannon rolled his eyes. Of all the stories she had to tell.

"Don't believe anything she says," he told her. He set his purchases on the counter and took a seat beside her.

"I thought it was funny," Joya remarked sweetly.

"I didn't," Evelyn said, her attention on Shannon. "You don't have to act like you have no home training just because you fall off the jungle gym."

"Ma, I was six. My arm was broken."

"And screaming like a banshee." She turned to Joya and said, "Two teachers and a nurse tried to help him, but he wouldn't let anyone touch him, wouldn't let anyone get near him. Just kept screaming for his mother. It got embarrassing after a while."

Joya smiled sympathetically at him. It wasn't the worst reaction to get forty plus years after the fact. But still.

"Alright Ma."

"I'm just saying. One day you'll have kids

and you'll see what I'm talking about," she said, glancing at him. "You'll see."

The comment struck Shannon. It had been a while since she made any inference about him having kids. It was common in his thirties, but nonexistent by the time he reached his forties, as if she understood what he did—kids were hard to come by when there was no spouse, no partner, no love interest.

Now she was talking about it again.

Hmm…

"Well, we should get started," Joya remarked, as she picked up her plate and walked it to the sink. She started to wash it, when Evelyn objected. "Just leave it, dear. You're doing enough for me already."

"I don't mind," Joya said. She finished what she was doing and set it in the dishrack. Then she dried her hands and turned around, ready to work. Shannon set his thoughts aside and got up. He showed Joya to the basement and the wall of junk his mother had collected over the years. Despite her objections, Evelyn was most definitely a pack rat and there was no way he was going to run everything by her first.

To her credit, Joya simply threw her chin up and said, "Great. I'll get started."

"You sure? There's still time to back out

if you want to."

"Yes. Go. I'll be fine. I got this."

"Okay. Just use your judgment. If it looks like junk, it probably is. Otherwise, we'll never get this house clean."

Joya acquiesced. Shannon went back upstairs. His mother was still at the table, an innocent expression on her face. She was up to something. Shannon thought to ask but knew she wouldn't fess up. He'd have to collect evidence first. He continued outside. It was already hot, but if he worked nonstop, he'd get done what he needed to do and spend the rest of his time inside.

With Joya…

No, making repairs…

Yeah, inside, where Joya is…

Inside the garage, Shannon collected the necessary tools and started on the back steps. They were in bad shape, literally. The corners were starting to peel, and the tops had lifted from their frames. It was a miracle his mother hadn't fallen before. Shannon worked on them until they were level, then turned his attention to the walkway. Part of him felt bad for letting the repairs go undone for so long. But he also understood, regardless of what he did, the house needed more attention than he could give it. It also didn't help that he wasn't the Mr.-Fix-It type either. His father, God bless his soul, was good with his hands, as was his grandfather, Big John. Somehow though Shannon was born without that gene; and no amount of practice or work pulled it out of him. As a young boy, he spent his summers on his grandfather's farm and the only thing he learned was how much he hated manual labor. He wasn't above it, but it wasn't his favorite thing.

Shannon chuckled as he considered what his grandfather would think of him now. He might express pride in his grandson's accomplishments, but more likely, he would think of him as less than a man for opting to work in an office. Despite this, Shannon missed the man. Big John wasn't the emotional type (unless he was drunk, of course), but he was loyal and cared for his family. It took him a while to accept Shannon as his grandson, but he did eventually care for him as much as he did his other grandchildren.

The white ones.

Shannon never begrudged his cousins and family members for being different, but it was difficult sometimes to accept that *he* was the odd man out. Even with his mother's side of the family. They were more accepting of him because he looked like them, but they never let him forget he was the son of a white man. Through all this, Shannon never complained, but he also never talked to his parents about it. Instead he struggled with his identity, struggled to make his own way in life.

Something he was still doing.

None of that mattered now. Times had changed and were still changing. It wasn't as a big deal to be of mixed heritage now, but the habits and thought processes were set. He dealt with the rejection, the loneliness and the scorn by being alone and doing things on his own. And because of it, his relationships suffered. Shannon hated to admit it, but he couldn't deny it either. More than once, he was accused of being *too* independent, or not trying hard enough. Even as awkward as his relationship with Trina was, he could have made it work. But he had given up on the notion of love, marriage and family a long time ago. This made it easier to talk himself out of his relationships. He liked to imagine that Joya would find him as attractive as he found her, but the truth was he'd find a way to sabotage that relationship and end up right back where he was—alone.

Shannon finished up the walkway and took a break. He sat on one of the steps he had fixed and leaned back, trying to find some shade from the sun's direct rays. He was drenched in sweat and ready for the day to be over.

The screen door creaked behind him. He turned around to see Joya coming outside, a couple of water bottles in hand. He made a mental note to add the door to his list of things to fix.

"Thought you could use something to drink," she said as she sat down beside him. Joya handed him a bottle, which Shannon gladly accepted. He took a long swig of the water then thanked her.

"How'd it go?" he asked.

"Fine," she said quickly, then sheepishly added, "Until I made the mistake of asking your mom about a box. She insisted on being helpful after that. I managed to convince her to lie down and rest, but she was adamant that she was going to help after getting up."

Shannon chuckled. That sounded like his mother. But in that, Joya handled her deftly. He was impressed. He chuckled once more then got serious for a moment.

"Listen, thank you for doing this—"

She interrupted him, her eyes on the bottle in her hand. "It's no problem really. I had the summer off—"

Shannon nudged her leg, so that she looked at him.

"No. Seriously. Regardless of whether you had the summer off or not, you didn't have to do this, and I appreciate it. Thank you."

She gazed at him for a moment, before she said, "You're welcome."

He nodded then took another long swig of his water, finishing it up.

"So, what do you have left for today?" she asked.

"I was going to look at the lights, but even those can wait until later." He sighed, allowing himself to feel pity for a moment. "I don't know, maybe if I had looked at all this before, she wouldn't have fallen."

Joya touched his arm.

"Don't do that. Don't beat yourself up for something you think you should have done. This wasn't your fault. This house is old. What happened was just an accident. Don't blame yourself."

He stared at her in earnest, astounded by her level of care for him. She wouldn't even let him wallow in pity. She was right. He stopped arguing.

"Yes ma'am," he responded. "Whatsoever you desire, my lady."

"That's what I like to hear," she said, seriously, then laughed. Shannon smiled. He liked the sound of her voice. It was melodic.

"I'll let you get back to work. Just wanted to make sure you were hydrated," Joya said, handed him the second bottle of water, stood up and went back inside. Without even trying, Shannon's heart followed after her.

He was in love.

Fourteen

IT TOOK JOYA A WEEK TO FULLY clean out Evelyn's basement. She thought Shannon was exaggerating when he called his mom a pack-rat, but when Joya started finding trivial items from previous decades, like used wrapping paper and packing boxes for greeting cards, she discovered he wasn't embellishing the truth at all. The woman saved everything. Joya understood Evelyn's hesitation to let go of her past, but a line had to be drawn somewhere. When she finally decided *not* to consult the older woman on anything, the work flowed easier and faster. By the start of the following week, she was ready to tackle the next project—the attic—which Shannon assured her was much worse. This was where Evelyn kept her actual keepsakes. Fifty years of memories, he told her. Regardless of what they found upstairs, Ms. Evelyn would not want to part with any of it.

Shannon, meanwhile, had made headway with the outer repairs and was working his way inside. Joya looked forward to having him beside her—he would be a better judge of what could go. Not just that though, she also enjoyed talking with him.

She enjoyed the companionship Shannon gave her.

After arriving at Evelyn's house, Joya knocked on the side door, then let herself in. Evelyn was old-fashioned in every sense and had insisted she didn't have to wait for someone to answer the door. Of course, the fact that it was unlocked posed another issue, but Joya didn't argue, knowing Shannon was around.

"It's me, Joya," she announced herself as she walked through the mud room and into the kitchen. Instead of Evelyn though, she found an older, black gentleman sitting at the kitchen table, eating. She stopped in her tracks, surprised to see him.

"Oh, hello," she said.

"Morning," he said, taking a big bite of toast.

"Is Evelyn here?" she asked awkwardly. She may have had permission to walk in, but she was still the stranger of the group.

"She's in her bedroom. Shannon ran out," he replied, then narrowed his eyes and asked, "You kin? I mean on Ole Jack's side."

"No, I'm not."

"You go to that bar on Sixth Street?" he asked.

"Uh, no."

He paused and looked her up and down.

"You were at the Summer Party…"

"Yes."

"I knew you looked familiar. And I usually don't forget faces. Listen here, I'm Trevor, Shannon's cousin," he said, standing up and offering her his hand. "I'm helping him out with the garage," he added.

"Nice to meet you, Trevor. I'm Joya," she replied, shaking his hand.

"Good, good." He sat back down and pointed towards the living room. "Go on in there. I'm sure Auntie will be happy to see you."

She thanked him and left. She continued towards Evelyn's bedroom, where she found her sitting on her bed, trying to get her socks on. Trying but failing. Joya could see the frustration mounting on her face.

"Let me help you," she said, effectively announcing herself.

Evelyn sat up at the sound of Joya's voice.

"Oh, hey Joya," she said and leaned back. The younger woman dropped her things on a nearby chair and walked over to the bed. She knelt in front of Evelyn and took the socks from her. "I know it's hot outside, but I get chilly walking on these hardwood floors," Evelyn explained.

"No problem. I'm happy to help." Joya

finished her task and looked over Evelyn's ankle. It was black in color, but the swelling had gone down. Evelyn didn't like to use her crutch and often leaned on the furniture or whatever was in her path to support her. When she wasn't walking, she propped up her leg, or iced it. She was taking things slowly and it was showing.

"You're looking better," Joya remarked.

Evelyn scoffed.

"You're just being nice now but thank you."

"I met your nephew, Trevor," Joya remarked, changing subjects.

"I asked him to help Jackie, since he's serious about me moving." There was a note of sarcasm in her voice. "Though I was hoping he would lose interest after a while," Evelyn added wistfully.

Joya touched her arm and gave her a gentle squeeze.

"I know it's hard, but it's in your best interest, so we can have you around for a few more years."

Evelyn didn't appear convinced.

"And what good is that if I don't have family?" she argued.

"You have family. You have Shannon. And you have me."

Evelyn gazed at her, seemingly

considering her words. The older woman eventually nodded and said, "I know, baby. And I thank you for everything you're doing." She patted Joya on her hand. "I'll let you do what you came to do. Did you eat? There's breakfast in the kitchen, if Trevor hasn't eaten it all. He takes after his father, my brother, and that man can throw down without competition."

Joya shook her head.

"I had some coffee this morning. I'm fine."

"You young kids. Jackie said the same thing," she remarked. "I'll let you get started then."

Joya left the room and started towards the attic. She hadn't ventured up there in all her time helping Shannon but figured it couldn't be any worse than the basement. Unfortunately, it was. There were trunks, boxes and bags everywhere. Joya didn't know where to start, but like everything else in life, nothing would get done until she did something. So, she chose a spot and began there. She found several bags of women's clothes that had become fodder for moths. Those could definitely go. Along with the shoes that had long worn out, and the women's hats that saw better days. Joya figured Evelyn had set it all aside until she could use them again, but that day never came.

Next, she came to a box of newspaper articles. Some were yellow and brittle with age. She handled them carefully, opening each one to see what kind of significance they held. The first one was an article on Shannon's accomplishments as the high school quarterback and football captain. There was a photo of him included with the text. He was much younger than the man she knew now, but she still recognized him. His eyes were the same—even back then they were kind and thoughtful.

Joya folded it up carefully and set it aside. She continued going through the stack, though more out of curiosity than work. Each article was about Jack, or Shannon, or a family member she had yet to meet. And each one was saved for a specific purpose. They were important to Evelyn and though Joya had no intention of throwing them out, she knew they wouldn't last much longer in the condition they were in. She thought about what she could do with them and decided to have them preserved in some way—a scrapbook, lamination, or something along that line. She'd figure it out later. Right now, she had to keep working. She skimmed through more articles and set them all in the same pile. When she got to the last one, she was surprised by its contents: it was about Michael and his accident. She didn't know the local paper had carried the story, but it would make sense, as this was his hometown. The paper was only a year old, but it touched her heart to see its place in with the others.

"She felt bad that she couldn't make the memorial."

Shannon's voice broke through her thoughts. She turned around and saw him standing at the doorway, watching her.

"Oh, hey," she said surprised to see him. "I thought you were working on the garage."

"I was. I am still. Just checking to see how you're doing since Trevor's taking a break," Shannon said and added, "Again. He's not the most reliable guy, but he's always willing to help. Especially for a beer."

"Sounds like my students—they'll do anything for a piece of candy but aren't much use after they get it."

He smiled at her, then walked over to her side. He looked at the article, and said, "They ran a series on him. Small-town hero and everything. Ma's probably got the other ones around here somewhere."

Joya looked down at it again, staring at the picture of her husband in uniform. He was a handsome man, regardless of what he was wearing. Or not wearing. She tried not to think of him in her waking hours, but it was when she was alone at night, accompanied only by her thoughts, that she missed him the most. Missed being with him, missed holding him, missed feeling him there with her, missed kissing him, missed hearing him. She even missed fighting with him, because in her mind, that meant he was still alive and still with her.

"He talked about you guys all the time," she finally said. "About his family back home."

Shannon continued searching through another stack of newspaper cuttings. He went through several before he finally found the ones he was looking for. He smiled at one then chuckled.

"You might like this one, I think. They interviewed a few of the guys he grew up with, who shared some stories Michael may or may not have told you."

Shannon passed it off to her and continued leafing through the pile.

Joya skimmed through the article, reading the memories the men shared of Michael. He had mentioned some of them to her before he died, but a couple were new. They brought tears to her eyes.

"He was a great guy. Hard to believe he's

gone sometimes. But I guess you know that more than the rest of us," Shannon said.

She nodded, not trusting herself to talk.

"I know he would appreciate the way you're taking care of his mom when you don't have to."

Joya straightened up.

"Gail has been a great mother-in-law," she said quickly. "I'd go anywhere with her."

"Like the Biblical Ruth?"

Joya shook her head dismissively.

"Hardly."

Shannon glared at her curiously, before saying, "Hardly? After all you've done for her?"

"She's done more for me, trust me. I'm not like Ruth."

"I don't know. I think I have a pretty good argument here, based on the evidence. This is my thing after all, lawyering and stuff."

She laughed.

"Ha, well I don't know about your thing, but—." She realized too late what she said and cringed. "That sounded dirty, didn't it?"

Shannon seemed amused by her.

"Oh, I don't know. I think it was sexy."

Joya blushed.

"Just forget I said anything," she pleaded.

"Well, you haven't actually said anything yet."

She frowned, confused by his comment. "About what?"

"Why don't you like to be compared to Ruth? This isn't the first time you've brushed off the comment."

Joya sighed. She didn't like talking about it, but since Shannon was asking...

"Because she could've gone home at any point. I didn't have that option." She paused, loathe to speak her next words. "My mother was raised to judge a person based on their skin color. She was brought up in a different culture and looked at men like Michael—and you—as beneath her. But that never made sense to me, you know? It's what's inside that matters. I tried to tell her that growing up but she was set in her ways. Nothing would change her mind. Then I met Michael and fell in love. I knew it was against everything my mom wanted for me, but I thought, once she meets him, she'll love him the way I do, and she'll stop judging. But it didn't work out that way. She refused to meet him. Told me she didn't want to see her daughter being tied down to one of 'those people.' And that I was much too good for 'his kind.' I had to choose—him or her." Joya took a deep breath and wiped the errant tears that had escaped. "Obviously, I made my choice, but I don't like making a big deal out of it. I don't like people thinking I made this grand decision, this great stand against prejudice and hate. I didn't."

"It takes courage to do what you did. I wouldn't be so quick to discount it," Shannon said gently.

She shook her head. "I chose love. That's an easy decision to make."

"I disagree. You're choosing one person over everyone you've known. That's not easy. You've got to be brave to do that."

"I suppose. And I suppose it was for your parents. But when I met Michael, it was like he was the answer I was waiting for, you know? He was…everything my heart wanted."

Shannon nodded understandingly.

"Were you ever in love?" she asked him.

"Me? Lots of times."

Joya didn't expect his answer. She knew he had never married, but assumed it was because he had never found anyone.

"I grew up with Evelyn Barton Reece," he stated matter-of-factly. "As tough as she is, she has the biggest heart of anyone in this county. My dad was a quiet man, not given to showy acts of affection, but he loved her till the day he died. So, I figured that would be my route in life—meet and fall in love with someone, like they did. I met and fell in love with several, beautiful women, even was engaged once."

"What happened?"

"Things didn't work out. No happily-ever-after."

"No," Joya agreed. She wanted to say more, but there was nothing else to be said. She wouldn't get her happy ending, any more than Shannon did. But it felt apropos that they be together, in the attic, sharing that.

"So how did you end up with Gail?" he asked.

"I couldn't go back home, and honestly, I couldn't fathom the thought of being alone, so I stayed with Gail after we moved back to the states. She had had a stroke a couple of years ago and I told her she needed someone to help her and care for her. She agreed, but I think she knew I was just scared."

The words were overdue. She could never speak them because they weren't becoming of her. Shannon didn't judge her for them though. He listened to everything she said; then took her in to his arms and held her as the tears fell and she succumbed to the emotions she had been holding in for so long. She would have felt horrified to have uttered those words to anyone, especially Gail, but being there with Shannon seemed to help her heart. She let him comfort her, let him love her.

Eventually she pulled back and wiped up

her face.

"I'm sorry, I didn't mean to get emotional," she said.

"Don't apologize. You're a lot stronger than you give yourself credit for."

"No. If I was, I'd be strong enough to just let all of this go."

"It takes time."

"No, the truth is I don't know how."

He took her hand and pulled her towards a chair over by the window. He encouraged her to sit, then sat across from her on a box.

"My grandfather had a heart attack when I was young. He survived, but he had problems afterward. Never fully recovered. The time came when we all knew he was going to die. I never cried in front of him, but I did that day Ma and Pa took me to the farm to say goodbye. He was still Big John, so he told me to dry up my tears, but what he told me afterward has stuck with me to this day. He said that my job after he passed was not to be upset but to remember him. That this was why we made memories, so we could continue to love and experience our loved ones after they were gone. It's not the same thing as having them with us, but if we allow it, our memories will heal our pain. Come on. What was your favorite memory of Michael?"

Joya gazed at Shannon. She wasn't sure what she was feeling, but there was something in his eyes and in his tone that soothed and calmed her. The tears still dropped but they were no longer flowing. They just were, while she tried to find the answer to his question. She had buried Michael deep inside her. Every time she thought of him, she only hurt and rather than explore the grief, she hid it back in her heart.

"It's not anything specific," she finally said, "But the way he would look at me when he got home at the end of the day or whenever he was away. Like he wanted to be there because he knew I'd be there. There was a trip he took before we married. He was due back at a certain time, but I couldn't be there. So, I went to his apartment ahead of time and cooked him dinner. I wanted to be sure he had something waiting for him. He told me later that even though he was glad to be back, he had wished I was there with him. That's when I knew his love was real."

"Well, my memories aren't quite as lovey-dovey," Shannon said. "Because I was older, I had to babysit Michael sometimes and I'll tell you, he was a piece of work, always into everything. One night when our parents were out, when he was about three, I made him go to bed because I was tired of babysitting. He kept saying he was thirsty, but I just kept telling him to go to sleep. He kept that up for a while before he finally quieted down. About an hour went by and I heard some noises in the bathroom. Found him in there dunking a hand towel in the toilet and sucking the water out of it. I guess he really was thirsty. I told him about it when he got older and said I would eventually tell his girlfriend. He punched me hard, actually knocked me to the ground. I deserved it I guess, but it's only right I keep my word. So now you know."

Joya laughed, harder than she meant to, but it helped her heart. And when she finally stopped, she hugged Shannon again. He felt right to her wrong, strong to her weak, and she wanted the healing he was offering her.

"Thank you," she finally said sitting upright.

"Hey, we're in this together, right?"

She nodded her agreement.

"I'm glad."

She was.

Fifteen

SHANNON DRAGGED HIMSELF out of bed, his mood already sour. He had been awake for a while, contemplating the day ahead of him, but could no longer put off the inevitable. Independence Day had finally arrived—and with it, the party he had agreed to in order to get his mother to move. Shannon was still against it, probably as much (if not more) as Evelyn was against moving; however, if he kept his word, then she was obligated to keep hers.

At least that's how it was supposed to work. Evelyn was not known for caving in when her mind was set on something; and the fact that she was still resisting efforts to finish cleaning and to talk to a realtor about putting the house on the market only confirmed in his mind that she was going to fight him, tooth and nail, when it finally came time to move.

With a grumble in his throat, Shannon got ready for the day. After showering up and getting dressed, he made his way downstairs to find the house was already bustling with activity. Trevor was back, and he had been joined by Kevin and Wyatt, two more of

Shannon's cousins from his dad's side. The three men were sitting at the table, eating breakfast.

"Hey guys," Shannon greeted them as he walked over to the counter to get a cup of coffee.

"Hey cuz," Kevin said.

Cup in hand, Shannon took a seat beside Trevor, who was washing down his eggs and bacon with a cold beer.

"Kind of early for that, isn't it?" Shannon asked.

"You have your poison," Trevor responded, pointing to his coffee mug, "I got mine."

Shannon changed the subject.

"You guys are here early, aren't you? The party doesn't start until later."

"Auntie called us," Kevin explained as he shoveled his eggs and grits into his mouth. "Said to get here early to help you set up," he added, though his words were hardly audible.

"And you know your mom, wasn't no arguing with her," Wyatt said.

Before Shannon could agree with them, Kevin interjected, his mouth still full, "So, Trevor was telling us about the girl?"

"What girl?"

"You know," Trevor said, nudging his arm. "That sweet Latin thing helping you."

Shannon raised an eyebrow.

"Joya?"

"Yeah that's her."

"Trevor said she's a looker, huh?" Wyatt said, a cheap smile on his face. Shannon didn't like where the conversation was going.

"Hot," Trevor added. "And single too. Thought I'd take a crack at her."

Shannon frowned, a little jealous.

A lot jealous.

Not that he imagined Joya could be charmed by Trevor or any of his other cousins, especially Kevin, who was now using his fork to pick food out of his teeth, but the fact that they might try something had Shannon ready to fight.

"She's not single, she's a widow," he stated more forcefully than he intended.

The three men looked at each other, then laughed. Heartily. At his expense.

"You still trying to be the knight-in-shining armor?" Kevin asked.

They had gone to high school together and while Kevin had his share of girls, Shannon had insisted on being a gentleman with the ladies. He had had one girlfriend to Kevin's six and they regarded that as a fault. Even now, thirty years later, they were still making fun of him for how he treated the fairer sex. Well, he knew how to shut them up.

"She's Michael's widow," Shannon stated firmly.

The laughter died down and the four men sat in silence, their faces somber, the mood dead. Kevin and Wyatt continued eating, while Trevor nursed his beer. They knew who Michael was and how he died, which meant Joya was off limits to them. Shannon was, of course, being a hypocrite, his waking thoughts filled with images of Joya, but he could live with that if it meant he didn't have to worry about competing with his cousins for her attention.

A knock on the door changed the ambience. Before any of them could get up to answer it, Joya walked in carrying a covered dish, Gail trailing behind her. Both women were dressed comfortably, but it was Joya who was garnering the most attention. The younger woman was wearing a tank top with yoga pants and her hair was pulled up in a pony tail. She wasn't wearing much make-up but even with the little she had on, she was gorgeous. Shannon noticed Kevin and Wyatt were staring at her with open mouths. It was not attractive, especially for Wyatt, who was married.

Joya smiled when she saw them.

"Oh, hello," she said sweetly.

Shannon stood up to help her, but Trevor

jumped in front of him.

"Here, let me get that for you," he said, taking the dish from her.

"Thank you," Joya replied.

Trevor smiled.

Shannon scowled at him before taking his seat.

"Auntie Gail," Kevin acknowledged, as he quickly rose to his feet and offered her his seat.

Gail shook her head and asked, "Thank you, no. Shannon, where's your mom?"

"In her room."

"I'm gonna go see if I can keep her out of trouble."

"Good luck."

After Gail left, Kevin offered his chair to Joya. Shannon wanted to kick himself for not doing it first.

"Thank you," she told Kevin as she took a seat.

"Can I get you some coffee?" Trevor asked.

"Or something to eat?" Wyatt asked.

Shannon didn't like what he was seeing.

"Coffee would be great, thank you," Joya replied.

While Trevor went to get her the coffee, Kevin sat down in Trevor's seat, his attention on Joya.

"Now I've met Trevor," she started in her

usual upbeat tone. Trevor seemed to beam that she had remembered his name. "But not you two," she added.

Wyatt stopped eating and offered her his hand.

"I'm Wyatt Reece. This is my brother, Kevin. We're Shannon's cousins. On his dad's side."

Shannon rolled his eyes. As if that wasn't obvious.

"Nice to meet you, Wyatt."

He was the one gushing now. Shannon wanted to throw up. They were making fools of themselves.

Like you didn't act that way when you first met her.

"Shannon was just telling us about you."

He sighed. Subtly was not their forte, but he knew Joya could handle whatever they said, especially when she glanced at him, winked, and asked, "Oh? I hope it was good."

"It wasn't enough nice things," Kevin said, as Trevor handed her a mug. She accepted his offering and smiled her thanks. He was beaming again. "We've heard how you've been helping Auntie Evelyn around here and getting the house ready for the move, because you're so selfless and just a great person…"

Yep, Shannon was officially embarrassed,

though not as much as Joya, who blushed at the accolades.

"Well, your aunt is a wonderful woman."

"Yep, yep," Kevin and Wyatt agreed.

"Of course, look at you guys, helping out with the festivities. I'm sure she couldn't plan this without you," Joya said.

"She would have found a way," Shannon muttered under his breath. No one seemed to hear him—they were too focused on Joya.

"We're always glad to help out. She called us this morning," Wyatt said. "And here we are, helping."

"Yep, that's us, just helpful."

"Well, I'm here to help too so put me to work," Joya stated.

Before his cousins could respond with anything inane or inappropriate, Shannon stood up and grabbed Joya's hand. "Actually, I was just about to pick up some stuff. Joya, why don't you join me?" he suggested. He didn't wait for her response but pulled her up so that she was standing. He didn't know if she had intended to stay or go with him, but he wasn't giving her a choice. Not with his cousins there.

"Alright. It was nice meeting you," she told them, letting Shannon guide her to the door, her hand still in his. "I'll see you later then."

Shannon could hear Wyatt say goodbye.

He quickly shut the door and showed her to his car. He released her hand to open the door and helped her in.

"So, what do we need to get?" she asked him as he got in and started the car.

He hadn't given any thought to it before suggesting the trip, but it didn't matter now that she was out of the house. Except he couldn't tell her that. They had to go somewhere now. His cousins had the hook-up when it came to alcohol. And if the invite list was anything like the last party, then that was all they would need. But he supposed they should have something to eat. His mother had been hosting these parties for so long, most people knew to bring food with them. There were some signature dishes she was known for, like her lasagna and her chocolate lava cake, but, because she was older now, she didn't cook like she used to. This was fine with most people, as they just wanted an invitation to one of her parties. This helped Shannon on the front end of the planning. But when all was said and done, it was the cleaning up that took most of the effort these days.

But Joya didn't ask any of that. She just wanted to know where they were going.

"We need to pick up some … incidentals … like … ice and cups and stuff," he said. He had gotten most of what they would need already, but these were items they usually ran out of, so it was a good idea to have extra on standby. "I also need to run by the office to pick up my laptop." That part wasn't a lie. Shannon had been checking his email on his smart phone, and though his clients were being handled by the other partners, he still preferred to do some work in the evenings, if only to feel productive.

Joya frowned at the mention of the detour.

"Are you sure you want me to come? I'm not exactly dressed for it."

His first thought was, *you look great*, but he didn't say it.

"It's a holiday, no one will be there," he assured her. Once they got to the office though, they were surprised to find Nathan there, working. The man was on a call, but when he saw them, he waved them in and quickly finished up.

"What are you guys doing here?" he asked, walking around his desk to greet them. "Shouldn't you be getting ready for your mom's party?"

Shannon groaned.

"Ugh, you're going..."

"She invited me," Nathan replied, matter-of-factly. "Called me personally."

"You don't have to go…"

"I can't say no to her."

"Try. Just a little bit harder. For my sake."

Nathan laughed, but gave no promise that he would. Instead he turned his attention to Joya, who appeared amused by the conversation.

"I hope Reece has been treating you alright these last few weeks. He tends to be a slave driver around here. Such a bear to work with," Nathan commented, though his tone was light and joking.

"He's been great," she said looking over at him. "Just a regular sweetheart."

Shannon was beaming now, just like his cousins.

"You know, that's exactly what I tell his clients, that he is a sweetheart," Nathan replied.

Joya laughed.

"Well, listen, you two, I'm gonna finish up here, then I'll see you later?" He looked at Shannon for confirmation, who nodded in agreement. "Oh, and listen, don't forget the open house this week."

"I haven't," Shannon assured him.

"Give me a call tomorrow and we'll hammer out any last details."

Shannon promised he would. He gave Joya a quick tour of his old office, then retrieved his laptop. When they returned home a couple hours later after running Shannon's fabricated errands, they found the party invitees had begun arriving. Shannon recognized family members from both sides, as well as church members.

"This was a terrible idea," he grumbled as they got out of the car and walked around to the trunk. "I should've never agreed to it. We're gonna have to start cleaning the house over again."

"Oh, stop," Joya reprimanded him, her tone serious, her hand on his arm for added emphasis. "This is her last hurrah. Leave her alone."

Shannon stopped and glared at her, aptly chastised, but also oddly turned on. That she felt comfortable and confident enough around him to rebuke him about his own mother was strangely sexy. He couldn't help the smile that creeped up on his face. Every argument he had about why he couldn't ask her out *(she's still grieving, she doesn't want you, you're too old for her)* went silent as courage rose up in him. Without so much as a second guess, he asked, "Joya, would you like to—?"

Sixteen

"IT'S ABOUT DAMN TIME YOU guys got back."

Joya turned around to see Kevin, Wyatt and another man descending upon them. He shared a familial resemblance to them and though she hadn't met him yet, she knew he was another cousin, or brother.

Pushing their way past Shannon, Wyatt and Kevin went through the trunk of the car, moving aside grocery bags, only to frown and grumble with disappointment.

"I thought you were bringing the kegs," Kevin remarked.

"We already have all this stuff," Wyatt added.

The third man was staring at Joya. He nudged Shannon in the arm and nodded towards her. With an embarrassed expression on his face, Shannon said, "Joya, this is my cousin, Brent. Brent, this is Joya." He seemed less than enthused to have to introduce them.

"It's nice to meet you, Brent," Joya said.

"Likewise," he replied, taking her hand in his and kissing it. "I've heard lots of good things about you."

Joya giggled, not because she was flattered, but because she could see Shannon roll his eyes.

"So, is this it?" Wyatt asked, pulling out the bags from the trunk and handing them to the others. It was a rhetorical question, because instead of waiting on a response, he turned to Joya and said, "You're probably tired after running all these errands. You want to grab a beer, or something to drink? We can go meet the rest of the family. Come on."

"I'm here to help though," she argued.

"Oh, don't worry about that," Brent replied. "Everything's covered."

"If you're sure," she said, looking from Brent to Kevin and Wyatt, who nodded in agreement. "Okay."

"Great," Brent said, taking her arm in his. Joya thought him a little forward but didn't say anything. She started following the others to the house, when she noticed Shannon wasn't with them. She turned back to see he was still at the car, closing the trunk, and looking a little lost. "Are you coming?" she asked him.

He looked at his cousins, then back at her.

"I need to check on Ma. Go, have fun. I'll be around," he said. "Go."

His cousins didn't wait to be told again. They dragged her to the house, dropped the ice and supplies off, then walked around, introducing her to the family and friends who had shown up early for the festivities.

"And this is where the magic happens," Kevin said, as they arrived at the grilling station. There were a couple of grills and a smoker going. Several men were sitting around on lawn chairs guarding their apparent kingdom. "You remember Trevor."

"Of course," Joya said.

Trevor smiled.

"And this is my brother George," Brent said, pointing to a man who looked like an older version of him. He touched her elbow and steered her attention to the others. "And this is Connor, Ryan, and Deshawn, Trevor's brother," he added. "Guys, this is Joya."

"Nice to meet you all," she said moving away from Brent and towards each man to shake their hands. "So, what's on the menu?" she asked, pointing at the grill.

"Name it and we got it," Deshawn replied, as he took a swig of beer. "Burgers, ribs, beef, pork, even some exotic stuff."

"Sounds good," she said.

"See what most people don't realize is that this is a science," Trevor said matter-of-factly. "The meat, the heat, the wood— different combinations get you different results. It's a beautiful thing."

He continued talking, sharing examples and techniques of grilling. Joya smiled politely, not wanting to discourage his interest, even if she had none. It was something she did with her students, but being surrounded by adults, she found she couldn't shake the boredom that was filling her thoughts. She enjoyed meeting Shannon's family, but wished he was there with her.

"I tell you, I could go on all day. You want something to drink?" Trevor asked.

"I'm fine," she replied. If she didn't get comfortable, she could leave. But they weren't having any of that.

"Here," Deshawn said, handing her a beer, as George turned to his brother and said, "Go get her a chair."

Brent appeared annoyed that he had been chosen to leave her side. With heavy sarcasm in his voice, he said, "Whatsoever you desire."

"What did you say?" she asked, curiously. She had heard Shannon say the phrase multiple times. She always meant to ask him about it, but never did. Now, hearing it come out of Brent's mouth, Joya had to know. Perhaps it was a family thing.

"It's something Ole Jack used to say to Auntie Evelyn," Trevor responded.

"The man was so in love with her, he

would have done anything she asked," Kevin explained.

"We just say it to be funny now," Brent said.

"No, *you* say it to be funny," George stated, slapping his brother across the head.

"That was *your* uncle. You should show more respect," Trevor chastised the younger man.

Brent glared at them confused, as if this was the first time he was reprimanded for saying it. Trevor shook his head in disappointment and continued giving Joya pointers about the grill. However, she was no longer listening. She knew how Shannon felt about his father. He wouldn't make fun of something he said, especially where his mother was concerned. So why would he say it?

Maybe it's something he says to everyone.

Try as she might though, Joya couldn't recall a time he spoke those words to anyone else; and she had spent a lot of time with him in the last few weeks.

You know why.

Joya's heart beat a little faster with the sudden realization that Shannon was taken with her. She could try to deny it, but it was obvious in the way he looked at her, the way he talked to her, his willingness to give her whatever it was she desired…

Obvious, but somehow, she missed it.

No, she argued. Didn't he tell her to remember Michael when they were in the attic? He wouldn't have done that if he wanted more. He was simply being a good friend. He was helping her heal.

For what? So he can ask you out?

Joya didn't believe that, not when the evidence was clear. Not when her heart was telling her otherwise. Shannon advising her to recollect the man she loved and had pledged her life to was a selfless thing to do, a thing borne out of friendship, but also love. She would have done anything, given anything to make Michael happy, to help him if he was down. Because she loved him. What Shannon did was no different. And the fact that he hadn't asked her out gave credence to that. He was giving her time, giving her space. That was love, pure and simple.

As a friend…and more.

Joya looked around the yard, searching for Shannon. She saw dozens of faces, many of whom she hadn't yet met, but none were him. He was probably inside, helping out. What was she hoping to see though? The look he gave her when his eyes rested upon her? Did she hope to hear his heart when he said her name? Or promised her whatsoever her heart desired? What was he going to ask her before his cousins interrupted him? Was he going to ask her out? Ask her to open her heart to him? Could she?

SHANNON HATED his cousins. They had not only interrupted the perfect moment but dragged Joya away from him. He would have to wrestle her from them if he was going to ask her out. That wasn't going to happen any time soon though. Shannon sighed and let the situation drop for the moment—he would see Joya again sometime later that evening. Or if not then, definitely after the party.

Shannon sighed, closed the trunk of his car and locked it up. Surveying the scene, he estimated at least a hundred people already in attendance. More would come. If anyone else was hosting any kind of get-together, his mother had easily eclipsed them. They might as well save themselves the trouble and just come over and celebrate with them. When he saw Ashley and Hannah coming over with a covered dish, he knew that's probably what his mother had done—invited everyone to eat and drink up all her food, then trash her house. If he was the suspicious type, he'd say she was sabotaging his efforts to sell the house, but he had no proof yet, so he held his tongue.

Hannah ran up to him and hugged him.

"Hi Mr. Shannon," she said holding onto his knees. He hugged her back. "My grannie came with us," she added with her usual excitement. "My peach grannie Margery."

Ashley approached with a woman who looked like an older version of her. They stood at about the same height, and both had the same fair skin and reddish colored hair. Ashley greeted him warmly then introduced her mother.

"I've heard so much about you and your mom," Margery said. Shannon could hear the levity in her voice. "*So* much."

"It's nice to meet you. We've heard quite a bit about you, too" he said jokingly.

Ashley blushed.

"We're gonna see the fireworks," Hannah announced, ready for the festivities. She made the sound of rockets exploding and waved her arms up and around. "We're gonna see all the lights and fireworks and they're gonna go in all erections and they're going to be pretty and—"

Ashley cut in, her face red, her eyes big.

"Oh my God, directions. She meant directions, directions."

Shannon wanted to laugh but held off,

seeing how embarrassed Ashley appeared.

"She also has trouble with the word 'truck'," the young woman continued. "So, if you hear her swearing later, that's what she's talking about."

It took Shannon a minute to understand what she was saying and this time, he laughed. Everyone joined in, including Hannah, who didn't seem to understand they were laughing at her.

Well, *with* her now. She seemed to have the uncanny ability to turn that around.

"Come on, I'll show you inside, get you out of this heat," he said. He led them to the house, then left them to help wherever he was needed.

As the afternoon wore on, family packed the house and gathered around to party. Music filled the air, as food and beer filled (adult) bellies. Unable to find anything else to do, Shannon joined his mother, who was inside the house, keeping cool. Gail and Margery were sitting with her along with several of the older family members, including a couple of aunts and his uncle Otis. They were laughing and enjoying themselves. Shannon walked in during a particularly boisterous laughter. He didn't announce himself, just remained in the background, listening. The only one who didn't look happy was Ashley. She had a mortified expression on her face and this time, it wasn't because of Hannah. The little girl was, in fact, outside, running around with some of Shannon's younger family members. No, this time the culprit was her mother, who was busy telling stories about her daughter.

"She was the most self-confident little girl you ever met. Couldn't tell her anything. Took credit for everything from potty training to teaching herself to tie her shoes."

"Mom!"

Margery ignored her daughter's plea.

"She went through this period where all she wanted to wear was her church outfits—you know the ones with all the frills and lace. Took to calling herself Diva. And when she figured out that wasn't high enough on the hierarchy scale, changed it to Queen of the Universe. Had all the other little kids in the daycare calling her that, wouldn't answer to anything else."

Laughter erupted again as Ashley's face went from a subtle pink to a blushing red. He felt sorry for her but was glad he wasn't the center of attention for once.

Ashley cleared her throat and stood up, even as the chuckling continued.

"I'm gonna check on Hannah."

Shannon gave her an understanding

smile as she walked by him.

The conversation continued but on a more serious note.

"I tell you what though, I always thought Ashley would conquer the world with that fearless attitude she had, but life beats it out of you and leaves you a shell of the person you once were."

"She seems to be doing fine," Evelyn said.

Otis lost interest in the conversation and went to the kitchen for another beer.

"She is now. And Hannah does her fair share to keep her on her toes. But it got bad for a while, especially with her relationship with the sperm donor."

Hannah's father, Shannon assumed.

"It'd be nice for her to meet someone who would treat her and Hannah right."

"Well, don't give up hope, Margery. There's someone out there for everyone. I mean look at me. Should have been impossible, but I found love in the most unlikely place. It's never too late. Sometimes they find it on their own, sometimes you have to give them a little push, show them what a jewel they have in that special someone."

Evelyn continued encouraging Margery. Shannon had stopped listening though. Why it only occurred to him now, he didn't know, but when she said the word 'jewel', Shannon knew—his mother wasn't trying to sabotage his work on the house…well, she probably was, but first and foremost she was trying to set him up…with Joya.

How could he have been so blind to her machinations? The parties, the hanging out together, the other women … the fall too? Shannon was sure that was just an accident, but he wouldn't put it past his mother to do something that extreme on purpose, simply to set him up with an available woman. He thought back to that day at the hospital. Was she acting any different?

No. But Gail certainly was.

You too, Gail? he thought. The woman was not the meddlesome type, so if she was involved, it was his mother's doing.

Still, as much as he didn't like his mother interfering with his life, Shannon found he wasn't as upset as he normally would have been. Because if Gail was involved in this matchmaking, then that meant they both saw something in Shannon and Joya worth bringing together. There was something there. His courage rose up again and he began anticipating the moment he would see Joya again. He was finally going to ask her out.

NIGHT FELL, and everyone gathered in the

yard where Brent had the fireworks ready for discharge. He was a safe distance from the house, but Shannon still cringed at the thought of all the damage his cousin could unintentionally afflict. Last year, he had managed to set the shed on fire. It was extinguished before any real damage could occur, but still, Shannon worried.

"Hey stranger."

Joya's voice cut through his thoughts and brought him back to the present. He turned around to see her lovely form approaching him. The smile on her face was enough to make him forget every subterfuge that was going on.

"Hey," he said, his heart beating a little faster. "Are you enjoying yourself?"

She walked up beside him and leaned against the railing of the deck.

"You have a great family. And yes, I am."

"I have an *interesting* family, you mean. It's okay, you can say it."

"Well, your cousin Brent did hit on me. And your uncle Leslie told me I needed to gain some weight because he likes his women thick."

Shannon said the only thing he could say when his family was involved.

"I'm sorry."

"No, it's alright. They're fun."

"You're being too nice."

She smiled guiltily, then stared out at the yard, where Brent was busy lighting up the first of the pyrotechnics. An awkward silence followed. Awkward only because of Shannon. He tried not to stare at her, tried not to think about his mother's meddling, or to look for any indication that she was right about Joya and him. His courage had dwindled some in the last few hours, but he was determined. He was going to ask her out. Right now.

"Oh, I saw your boss," Joya said.

Opportunity lost. Nathan had eventually found his way to the house, and after flirting with Evelyn and all of Shannon's aunts, had decided to party. Last time Shannon saw him, he was passed out on the front porch.

"Listen, Shannon...," Joya started, looking back at him. Then the first of the fireworks went off. It whistled as it shot into the sky, then exploded into millions of lights and colors. Joya followed the trail with her eyes, her face as lit up as the sky. And though everyone else's attention was on the fireworks, Shannon found he couldn't take his eyes off of Joya. She was stunning.

Joya turned to him again, the lights reflecting in her eyes. Her smile didn't disappear but morphed into something else, something curious, something more. Was it want? Desire? A reflection of all the things he sought? She fixed her gaze on him, the fireworks going off, one by one, whistling into the sky, then bursting into lights and sound. Shannon found himself drawn to Joya. He leaned forward and closed the space between them. All noise around them seemed to die down and all people seemed to disappear, leaving just him and her. He closed his eyes and prepared to kiss her, but just as he was about to set foot in heaven, Joya pulled away from him.

"I'm sorry," she said, and walked away.

Seventeen

THE FIREWORKS CONTINUED, even as Joya found the bathroom and locked herself in. Her heart was thundering in her chest and tears were streaming down her face. She stared at her reflection in the mirror.

What are you doing?

She had begun to say something, to ask him how he felt about her, but then she got lost in his eyes. What was she doing? Why was she entertaining this with Shannon, of all people? He was her friend. He was the rock that kept her steady. He had filled the empty holes that would otherwise have remained empty. So why was she doing this?

Because of what you saw in his eyes.

Indeed, there was something about him that reminded her of Michael, of the love and desire she saw in his gaze when he looked at her. Now Shannon was offering the same thing. And for a moment, she wanted that—his love, his attention, his effort. She wanted to feel love again, to know love, to share that with someone. No, to share that with Shannon.

Joya wasn't ready for anyone to take Michael's place though. She let her emotions lead her, let herself think she was interested and ready. She wasn't sure if she would ever be though and she didn't want to hurt Shannon by letting him believe there could be something between them. He was too important to her.

There was a knock on the door. It was quiet, so as not to be noticed by others, only her. She knew it was Shannon, knew he was checking in on her after she immaturely ran away from him and left him on the deck.

God, what he must think of her.

Another knock. Joya hesitated—a moment longer than she thought Shannon would stay. Then she panicked because she thought he wouldn't. She unlocked the door and stood back, unable to open it. Shannon cracked it open, as if to make sure it was her, then let himself in. He shut the door and leaned back against it.

"Joya, I'm sorry. I overstepped my bounds," he said with penitence in his voice.

She shook her head vehemently. She wasn't going to let him take the blame on this.

"Don't. I'm the one who should be sorry. I shouldn't have let it go that far."

There was a momentarily wounded expression on his face, but he straightened up and said, "No, the truth is, I got lost in the idea that you and I could be something more.

I didn't mean to push you into something you weren't ready for."

"Shannon, please—"

"No, it was a lapse of judgment on my part and I'm sorry."

Joya sighed. She knew what she wanted to say, but it seemed inappropriate.

"Please don't do that. I'm just as responsible. You've been an incredible friend to me and the truth is, I let you love me, without giving you anything back in return—"

"That's not true—"

"Shannon, I *love* you, but it's not in me to fall in love again."

Perhaps she was wrong to tell him that, but she couldn't go forward if he didn't understand what she truly felt for him.

Shannon shook his head as if to argue, but he didn't say anything. She couldn't read his thoughts, but she could see how her words affected him.

"So, what happens from here?" he finally asked her.

"Can I ask you to continue being my friend? I know this is selfish on my part, but I don't want to give that up."

"Neither do I," he told her, softly. He stood up off the wall and took a couple of steps towards her. "I value your friendship."

She smiled appreciatively and met him

halfway. She wasn't sure if she made the first move or if he did, but they hugged. She held onto him, as he held onto her. It wasn't the same as before though.

"YOU'RE QUIET," Gail told her as they got into the car at the end of the night. It was well-past two o'clock in the morning and while many of the guests had gone home, some, like Shannon's cousins, were still celebrating.

"I'm just tired," Joya replied honestly. She wasn't sure if it was the partying or the emotions that wore her out, but she couldn't wait to get home, crawl into bed, throw the blankets over her head and go to sleep.

Gail talked for a few minutes about the party, but she fell quiet after a while and the rest of the ride home was spent in silence. When they got home, Joya helped her mother-in-law out of the car and into the apartment. They got ready for bed and turned in with only a brief 'goodnight'. Joya tried to rest, but she couldn't fight the dark emotions settling over her. Not wanting to be alone, she got up and climbed into bed with Gail. The older woman turned around and looked at her.

"What's wrong, baby?"

Joya knew her mood was obvious. It was

a fine balance in the past, being strong, hiding how she felt so she could be the shoulder Gail leaned on. Tonight, though, she didn't think she could do this on her own.

"I miss Michael," she said quietly.

Gail didn't say anything, simply put her arm around her and hugged her. Joya didn't cry, just let the older woman comfort her; and tired as she was, she eventually fell asleep.

Joya slept in the next morning. When she finally awoke, she found she was alone—Gail had gone to an appointment. Joya had the place to herself. She thought about just relaxing in bed, but she was never the type to do nothing. She got up, washed up and brewed some coffee. She sat down in front of the television to catch the news, but try as she might, she couldn't pay attention. Her thoughts kept going back to the prior evening. She remembered Michael's face when she talked to him and the reaction he gave her.

Shannon, not Michael.

She thought about *his* reaction and *his* willingness to keep their relationship platonic. About her first kiss with Michael, about her first time being intimate with him. About her loneliness. About her desire for Shannon.

Joya shook the thoughts off. They were getting jumbled up, confusing her. Maybe it was because of all the time she was spending with Shannon that she was thinking like this. Or because she was thinking about Michael instead of trying to think about other things. Regardless, she had to get a handle on herself, especially if she was going to return to Evelyn's house. She had told Shannon she would take the next day off because she wanted to rest and look after Gail, but she needed some distance from Shannon. She needed to get her thoughts together before she saw him again.

She wondered for a moment if Shannon was thinking about her. Would he care if she wasn't there? Or even notice?

God, what was wrong with her?

Joya turned the television off, got dressed and went out, determined to put both Shannon and Michael out of her mind. She went to the gym. Then, because the day was only half over, she went to the store and picked up some items to finish the scrapbooks for Evelyn. She had spent the last couple of weeks on them, carefully preserving each article in their own archival plastic sleeve and organizing them by date. It was a lot of work, but she enjoyed doing it. She returned home with her purchases to find Gail was back, sitting at the kitchen table, enjoying a cup of tea.

"How was your appointment?" Joya asked as she put her purse and bags on the counter.

Gail smiled.

"Good," she said. "How was your day? Are you feeling any better?"

Joya thought about Shannon for the first time since that morning. She couldn't say she was feeling better, but she wasn't as anxious as she was before. Part of her knew the less she thought about Shannon, the better she would fare.

"I'm fine. Really," Joya said as she joined Gail at the table. She hated that she had said anything about how she was feeling, especially about missing Michael and insisted, "It was just a moment."

"I understand, baby," Gail said, patting her hand. "I just want to be sure you're okay."

"I am," Joya assured her.

Gail gazed at her for a minute. She didn't appear to be convinced, but she let the subject go.

JOYA RETURNED to Evelyn's house the next day, bringing the scrapbooks she had completed with her. There were several large ones, and a few smaller ones, all packed into a file box. Though her hands were full, Joya knocked, then entered, announcing herself as she walked through the mudroom and into the kitchen. None of this was any different than she had done in the past. This time though, when she saw Shannon sitting at the kitchen table, eating breakfast, her thoughts returned to their jumbled state and it wasn't a smile she greeted him with, but a mouth agape with uncertainty.

Shannon offered her a small smile and stood up.

"Morning. Here, let me help you," he added, wiping his hands on a napkin and taking the box from her.

"Thank you," she replied and handed him the box. She forced herself to smile back. "Those are for your mom. I took all those clippings she had and some of the old photos and organized them."

Shannon set the box on the table. He took the lid off and carefully inspected the books.

"This is great," he said, with admiration in his voice. "She'll be very happy."

Joya smiled her thanks but didn't say anything else. She watched him as he replaced the lid and moved the box to an empty chair on the other side of the table. He looked at her. There was something unspoken between them—or something that needed to be spoken. She couldn't tell the difference, if there was one. It was just awkward.

"Did you eat?" he asked her. "Coffee?"

"Yes, please," she replied quickly, then

took a seat at the table, happy for the distraction. Shannon grabbed a mug for her and filled it with coffee. Then he added the amount of sugar and creamer she liked. She thanked him and focused on the drink in front of her.

God, why was this so hard? She was an adult, she could handle this.

Joya took a deep breath.

"So, the house is still standing," she quipped.

"Barely," he remarked, as he sat back down. "I love my family, but they leave a mess everywhere they go."

Joya saw the scorch marks on the back lawn when she drove in and there was wood piled up by the front porch where the railing and support were missing.

"I'm sorry I didn't stay behind the other night to help," she said.

"I didn't expect you to. They're my kin."

There was no tone in what he said, but Joya felt bad anyway. She decided to change the subject.

"How's your mom doing? I bet the partying wore her out."

Shannon nodded in agreement.

"She still acts like she's superwoman sometimes. She needs to slow down."

Joya was the one who nodded this time,

but when she went to follow up, she found she had nothing to say. Nothing worthwhile anyway. It was all small talk, empty words to fill the empty space between them. Apparently, Shannon didn't have anything else to say either, because he went back to eating breakfast. Suddenly Joya wished she could leave and go back to the safety of her home. She wished she had never volunteered to help Shannon, wished school was starting today so she didn't have to spend any more time with him, wished things could go back to the way things were before the summer started and she spent so much time with him. It had her hoping for things that ought not be and now, it had ruined their friendship.

As if reading her thoughts, Shannon looked up at her, took a deep breath and said, "Listen, I think once we pack up the last of the things that need to go to the storage unit today, we'll be done here. I can take care of the repairs on my own. You've been a big help and I don't want to take up anymore of your summer."

Joya would have normally argued, said it wasn't a problem, insisted she was happy to help. Not today though. He was giving her a pass, most likely because he was feeling the same thing.

"Okay," she said and left the situation at that.

Eighteen

SHANNON PUT THE LAST OF THE boxes into the storage unit and closed it up. He didn't think it was possible, but they had finished packing up his mother's things. Granted, there was still a way to go—repairs to be made, a house to clean up, furniture to get rid of, but the most important part was done and that's what mattered.

Shannon locked up the unit and returned to his car. It was already dark outside, his day spent getting everything into his car to transport. Still he felt a sense of accomplishment and that was worth it. Or it would have been, had things turned out different with Joya. Following the party, he knew it would be hard seeing her, but he never imagined how difficult it turned out to be. He regretted trying to kiss her almost immediately. Obviously, she wasn't ready—or interested—and it ended badly for him; and though they had agreed to remain friends, even that didn't seem possible anymore. Maybe all they needed was time, then they could return to what was. Shannon just wasn't sure he could be happy with that anymore. He was in love with her and the thought of being around her without being able to express that...

Shannon opted not to think about Joya anymore and drove home—his home. Even though his mom was still in a cast, her ankle was better, as was her mobility. He made sure she had no need for anything in the basement, or upstairs, but he also knew that wasn't going to stop her from going where she wanted to go or doing what she wanted to do. This made his efforts pointless …

Duly frustrated with the women in his life, Shannon chose not to think about her either. When he arrived at his apartment, he showered and changed into a pair of sweats and t-shirt. Then he sat down on the couch with his laptop to focus on work. Shannon scanned the emails. Client. Nathan. Client. Coworker. Spam. Lots of spam—from the obligatory foreign prince who wanted to email him millions to the performance enhancers that would help him with the ladies. Those were nothing though compared to the next one: single seniors looking for other single seniors. He had gotten them before, when he was younger and on the verge of hitting the half-century mark. They were laughable then, but now that he was on the other side of fifty, it wasn't so humorous. Because that's who he was and that's who the world saw him as. Perhaps he should have garnered some hope that even at his age it was possible to find love, but given his track record, he wasn't likely going to get a happily-ever-after.

Shannon closed his laptop and went to bed.

"HEY MA, it's me," he announced as he walked into his mother's home. She was sitting at the kitchen table, eating breakfast. Her arm was resting on the table, her leg on the chair in front of her.

"Hey Jackie," she said and held her head up for him to kiss her. He obliged, then took a seat beside her.

"How're you feeling this morning?" he asked her.

"I'm fine."

"How's your leg? You're not walking on it too much, are you?"

Evelyn let out a noisy breath.

"Son, I love you, but you need to stop treating me like an invalid. I'm fine. I'm healing. I'll be back to my usual in no time," she said with a certain edge to her voice that told him she wasn't in the best mood.

Shannon threw his hands up and said, "Sorry for caring."

She ignored his comment and looked past him.

"Where's Joya?"

Shannon wanted to roll his eyes, as he

thought about the real reason she was asking. He took a deep breath instead and said, "She's not coming."

Evelyn's eyebrows shot up.

"Why not?"

"We're done."

"What do you mean, you're done?"

"With the house. We're done packing up. I've got some repairs to make from the party but after that, you're moving in with me."

"I'm not moving," she exclaimed.

Shannon had anticipated this argument, but he wasn't in the mood for it today.

"You agreed to move if we had one last party," he said through clenched teeth.

"I'm not moving," she reiterated, defiantly.

"This house needs more work and money than you and I can put into it."

"So, what, we just give up on it? Is that what we do when we get old and beyond use?"

"You're being unreasonable, Ma."

"Well, I'm telling you I'm not moving. I appreciate everything, but I'm not going."

"Then why did you say yes?" he asked, exasperated.

"Because I thought you and Joya would have gotten together by now."

Shannon let out a contentious laugh.

"Ah, yes, your master plan."

Evelyn stared at him confused.

"What?"

"You didn't think I'd figure it out?" he asked, his tone more bitter than he intended. "That you were trying to set me up with Joya?"

"A lot of good it did me, huh? You're still single and now I'm out of a house."

"You're not out of a house, you're gonna live with me."

Evelyn didn't want to hear him though. She set her leg down on the ground and used the table and chair to support her as she stood up. She walked over to the sink, muttered something incoherent to herself, then turned back around, ready to fight.

"Are you gay, Jackie? Is that it?"

"What?"

"You can tell me. You're my son. I'll love you regardless of who you're attracted to. You should have told me years ago, so I could make alternate plans for grandchildren, but I'll still love you."

"Are you being serious right now?"

"Why is this so damned hard for you then? I don't get it. I met and married your father when I was young and when it was impossible. And here you are, fifty and still alone, living in a world your father and I only dreamed about. I don't understand."

Shannon got up, flustered. He moved

towards the mudroom, unwilling to look at his mother right now. He didn't want to argue, but he couldn't *not* respond, because it would only postpone the inevitable. Then he'd have to have this conversation again. He turned back around and glared at Evelyn, who was watching him expectantly. Apparently, she didn't want to postpone the conversation either.

"I appreciate the example you and dad set for me, but it's not as easy as you make it out to be. Do you think I want to be alone? Don't you think I want to find someone to settle down with?"

"I don't know. You were always so independent—"

"I had no choice! No one wanted to be seen with the little half-breed kid. I had to be independent and do things on my own," he exclaimed, then forced himself to calm down. "Eventually, it just became easier to be alone."

Evelyn didn't immediately respond. She just stared at him, regret in her eyes.

"I knew others gave you a hard time," she eventually said, her tone apologetic, "But I always thought you were just more like your father. He was always off doing things on his own, happy to be by himself and then come home…" The edge dropped from her voice.

"Why didn't you tell me?"

"Because of the way you're looking at me now," he replied, the fight gone from him.

She sighed loudly and walked back to the table.

"You didn't have to go through that alone," she said.

"I know. But it's too late for that."

"Times have changed."

"Yeah," he acknowledged.

"What about Joya? She was married to Michael, so obviously those differences don't matter to her."

Shannon sat back down at the table.

"Look, Ma, it's just not going to work."

"Well, have you asked her out?"

"No," he replied truthfully.

"Then ask her out."

"Please just leave it alone."

"I can't. Not when I've seen the way she looks at you."

"You're reading into things."

"There's love there."

"Leave it alone please."

"You've got to claim your stake."

"That's not the problem this time."

"What do you mean?"

She stared at him, waiting for clarification, but the last thing he wanted to do was to admit he had been rejected. Mustering up the firmest voice he could, Shannon said, "Ma, I love you, but you need to stop meddling. Just let this be."

Nineteen

OF COURSE, EVELYN COULDN'T do that, not where her only child was involved. It was plain to see how smitten he was with Joya; and anyone could see that Joya was just as besotted with him. For whatever reason though, they weren't connecting. Evelyn had to fix that.

Unfortunately, Jackie wasn't letting her out of his sight. They had finished up their conversation, but he was still hovering over her, making sure she was okay. But also, making sure she wasn't trying to sabotage his plans because she was and they both knew it. While it was always her plan to throw a party for the holiday, she knew that with all the people who showed up, setbacks were inevitable. This was why she insisted on celebrating there. There wasn't a whole lot of damage, compared to previous years, but it was enough to delay Jackie. Her drunk brother put a hole in the kitchen wall. Jack's cousin fell off the porch and broke the railing. Her nephews set the backyard on fire with the fireworks. It hurt her heart to see the damage to the house her beloved Jack built her, but it served its purpose. Now, though, she was almost out of time. She had to call Gail.

Evelyn preferred to go see her friend, but she had never driven with a cast before, and she was sure Jackie wouldn't let her go by herself. Then instead of hovering over her, he'd be hovering over *them* and they wouldn't be able to plot effectively. She could try to sneak a phone call, but with Jackie in the house, she'd likely have to cut the conversation short. No, she'd have to find another phone to use. One with more privacy, and as she peered out the window and saw Hannah playing in her yard, she knew she'd found her answer.

Evelyn got herself ready and put together a plate of cookies and treats for the little girl and her mother. With such a fine offering (or bribe), Ashley wouldn't mind if she borrowed the phone while Evelyn was visiting with them.

"Where are you going?" her son asked as she limped through the kitchen with her purse hanging on her arm and the plate of cookies in hand. He was working on replacing the drywall where her brother had damaged it.

"Going to visit with Ashley."

He stopped what he was doing and brushed his hands off.

"I'll take you."

Evelyn took in a deep breath and in her

most cantankerous voice, said, "I didn't ask you to take me."

"Your ankle is still not strong enough. I don't want you getting hurt."

"You're the one who's going to be hurt if you don't let me live my life."

Jackie made a face—the one he usually reserved for her whenever she had gotten on his nerves—and stepped back. Without another word, he went back to the wall.

Satisfied, Evelyn proceeded out the door, with her head held high. She walked down the driveway to the street, still strong, still able. However, Jackie was right about her ankle. She hadn't put much pressure on it in the past few weeks and now it was objecting to the forced activity. Nonetheless, she persisted, knowing everything that was at risk.

Hannah saw Evelyn and ran across the neighbor's yard to meet her. She greeted the older woman with an enthusiastic hug. As happy as Evelyn was to see her though, she was quick to correct her.

"Don't be running off like that, okay?" she said, in between breaths. "You could get hurt or in a lot of trouble."

Hannah let go of the older woman, looking aptly repentant.

"But I wanted to see you," she argued.

"And I wanted to see you too, sweetheart, but you have to be safe first, okay?"

Hannah nodded.

"Good. Now is your momma home?"

"No. Mommy's working. Gramma Margery is home."

Well, that would work too. She and Margery had hit it off the other night. The woman would be happy to help her. And indeed, she was.

"That was quite a little shindig you had the other day, Ms. Evelyn," she said, opening the door for her. "Come on in."

"Thank you, thank you," Evelyn said, as she entered. She moved to the nearest couch and sat back, only too happy to get off her feet. She thought about making small talk, but Evelyn didn't have the patience—or the breath—for that right now. "Can I borrow your phone?"

Margery said yes and was gracious enough not to ask questions. It was Evelyn's plan to tell her everything, but first, she had to talk to Gail and find out what was going on. Unfortunately, the woman was home with Joya and couldn't talk.

"Can you meet somewhere?" Evelyn asked her.

"I suppose."

"Good. Meet me at the diner downtown."

Evelyn hung up, content with herself. Then realized she had no way of getting there. She turned to Margery, who was quietly watching her, and asked, "You up for a little road trip? I have gas money and cookies."

GAIL PARKED her car in the diner's lot and turned it off. She wasn't feeling well today. Between the pain and the nausea, she would have preferred to stay home and rest, but Evelyn's tone was urgent. She couldn't say no.

Gail exited her car and slowly made her way to the door of the diner. She saw Evelyn sitting in a booth, accompanied by Margery and Hannah, all of whom were indulging on pie, cookies, coffee and juice. Evelyn saw her and waved her over. She wasted no time getting to the purpose of the meeting.

"What happened?" Evelyn exclaimed. "Between Jackie and Joya? Everything was going so well, then it wasn't."

Gail eyed Margery hesitantly, as if Evelyn was breaching their confidence by including her in the conversation. Well, her and Hannah, but mostly Hannah, since the little girl liked to talk.

"Don't worry. I explained everything to

her," Evelyn assured her. Margery nodded in agreement, her countenance as anxious as Evelyn's to hear more about the situation. "And Hannah is not going to say anything, right?"

The little girl nodded enthusiastically as she filled her mouth with pie.

"So, did Joya say anything?" Evelyn asked.

Gail thought about the young woman's reaction in the last few days, but nothing seemed out of the ordinary. She had had a moment where her grief became too much to bear alone, but Gail had been there before.

"Nothing," she replied. "Everything's been normal."

"Maybe something happened at the cookout?" Margery offered.

Evelyn shrugged her shoulders.

"I don't know and Jackie's not talking to me. It's obvious he's crazy about Joya, and I've seen the way Joya looks at him, but something's preventing them from connecting. We've got to do something or I'm out of a daughter-in-law and a house."

"What else is there?" Gail asked. She had gone to Evelyn for this reason: she wasn't good at planning, plotting or matchmaking. In fact, it was a good thing Michael had found Joya, because there was no way Gail would have had the wherewithal to set him up with anyone.

"They're done cleaning up the house. My family, God bless them, bought us a little time when they trashed the place, but that's not anything Jackie won't have fixed up by next week. Joya said something about joining a book club, but my son's not a reader. He's got his work thing tomorrow, the open house they're having in his honor. Perhaps she could crash it. But again, if they're not connecting, I don't know how we'd get her there, or what good it would do if she did show up." Evelyn stopped, and looked to her friend with a lost expression on her face. "Honestly, Gail, I don't know," she admitted.

The three women sat in silence, staring at each other for some kind of direction. Only Hannah continued as she was, eating with loud, audible bites.

"There's always the direct approach," Margery ventured.

It seemed like the obvious answer, but there was a reason they had made it a clandestine affair—Shannon and Joya would fight it.

Evelyn sighed, as if she was thinking the same thing. She turned to Gail and said, "Hell, we've tried everything else." She then seemed to remember Hannah was sitting with them. She turned to the little girl and told her, "Sorry. Don't say that word."

Hannah nodded obediently.

"I don't know if that'll work," Gail interjected. She thought about all the times she tried to talk to Joya, only to have the woman brush off any grief or emotion she might be feeling. Gail wasn't blind, she knew her daughter-in-law was acting strong for her, and it was selfish of her to let her do it. Both had lost much and they *both* needed someone to lean on. But Joya had taken that role on to the point where she wasn't letting anyone in.

"Well, we'll have to make it work. Or *you* will. You need to talk to her."

"Me?"

"You know her best," Evelyn insisted. "I talked to Jackie and he all but admitted his feelings for her. But that's as far as he's willing to take it. So now, you have to talk to her."

Gail grimaced. She was never one for direct confrontation.

"There's interest there, Gail," Evelyn maintained when she saw her wavering. "If she can take the lead, then Jackie will follow suit. That's the way love works. My Jack might not have married me, not with that father of his. I had to get off my ass and ask him." She turned to Hannah, and added, "Don't say that word either."

"Okay," the little girl replied.

"Ashley's father was the same way," Margery agreed. "He kinda coasted through life, letting things just happen. It wasn't until I made the first move that he made his."

"Just talk to her, Gail," Evelyn said, softening her tone. "My house aside, this could be their chance at true love. I know Joya had it with Michael and she was a good wife to him, but Michael wouldn't want her to be alone. If she's just not interested in my son, so be it. But if there's even a snowball's chance in hell—remember not to say that word—that Joya is, then we have to help them see it before it's too late."

Gail sighed and nodded her agreement.

"I'll talk to her."

"Good," Evelyn said, as she grasped her friend's hand and squeezed it.

Margery added her hands to theirs and suggested, "So, listen, when you two finish up with Shannon and Joya, maybe we can discuss you finding someone for Ashley."

Twenty

WITH DINNER DONE, JOYA sat down on the couch to watch television and wait for Gail, who had run off on an unexpected errand. She flipped through the channels until a trashy romance movie caught her attention. She didn't normally watch these types of films as they were more drama than romance, but found it was a like a train wreck—no matter how hard she tried, she couldn't turn away. She should have been catching up on one of the books she borrowed from Sarah, as she was now back to filling her time with reading until school started, but she wasn't feeling it right now. She wasn't feeling much of anything lately.

Gail came home about halfway through the movie. Joya turned the television off and greeted her mother-in-law.

"Did you get what you needed?"

Gail nodded. Without a word, she placed her purse on the counter and walked over to the couch. She appeared more tired than usual, but she didn't complain.

"Let's talk, Joya," she said.

There was a gravity in her tone that Joya couldn't ignore. Had something happened while she was out?

"Is everything alright?"

Gail didn't answer Joya's question, but sat down on the couch beside her. She took her hand and held it between hers.

"You know you've been a blessing to me, right?" she asked, looking up at her.

"Yes."

"And I know you were a loyal and loving wife to Michael."

Joya pulled her hand away and looked down, knowing what was coming.

"Baby, look at me," Gail said softly.

Joya was usually obedient in that respect, but she couldn't comply, not this time. Not when she knew what Gail was going to say.

"Joya, please."

"I'm fine," Joya remarked, but didn't look at her mother-in-law. Instead, she gazed down at her hands, now resting on her lap. "The other night was just a moment."

"I know. I've been there too. There were times I missed Earnest so much, I thought the emotions would crush me. And he's been gone for much longer, so believe me when I say, I understand. I'm not judging you on that."

Joya turned to the older woman.

"Then why do you keep bringing this up?"

"Because I want you to live your life to

the fullest."

"I am."

"No, Joya, you're not."

"I am," Joya insisted. She loved Gail, but the woman was wrong. Her life was full. It wasn't perfect, but she was okay with where she was.

"You should be happily married and taking care of children, not an old woman who's not even your mother."

"Don't do this. You know if Michael was here—"

"But he's not. Worse than that, the moment he stopped living, so did you."

Joya had no response for that. Deep down inside she knew Gail was right.

"You're going through the motions, Joya. You're existing, looking for something to distract you from the memories, but you can't continue like this. You have to start living again. You have to start enjoying life. You have to start loving again."

"I do," Joya insisted, her eyes stinging with unshed tears. "I love you."

Gail shook her head.

"Not me."

And though Joya could deny it to her dying breath, she knew whom Gail meant— Shannon. She had scarcely been able to get him out of her mind. She had tried, so very hard, but couldn't; and it scared her.

The tears fell now, no longer hindered by her own denial. She was scared, plain and simple; scared to love, scared to open herself up to the vulnerability of loving once again.

"Joya, what happened? At the cookout?"

Joya thought about Shannon, remembered the tender expression in his eyes, on his face when he looked at her. The love he had shown her in the weeks they spent working together.

"He...we started to kiss," she admitted quietly, "But I turned away from him."

"Do you love him?"

Joya dropped her gaze.

"Yes."

"As a friend?"

"Yes."

"More?"

Joya opened her mouth to say 'no' but found she couldn't respond.

"Are you in love with him?"

"I can't be," Joya uttered, her voice barely audible even to her ears. "I can't be. I'm still in love with Michael."

Gail turned Joya's face towards her and offered her a tender, understanding smile.

"You were a good wife to my son, loving and loyal, the best anyone could ask for, but he's gone."

"Not from here," Joya exclaimed, resting

her hand on her heart.

"And he never will be, but you can't let that stop you from loving again. Joya, listen to me. You have that opportunity, to love, to be in love, to be loved. You deserve it. But you have to give yourself permission to do that. You have to make that choice. Whether it's Shannon, or someone else, you deserve to be loved."

Joya said nothing, her heart breaking all over again. She wanted everything Gail was saying. She wanted to love, to be loved, but her chance for that ended with Michael. Her chance, her world, her life ended when he did.

Tears continued streaming down her face.

"I'm sorry, sweetheart," Gail said as she gathered her into her arms for a hug. "I didn't mean to make you cry. I just want what's best for you."

Joya didn't fight the embrace but let herself be enveloped by it. She had always tried to be a comfort for Gail, but now she could see she had been denying herself the same thing. She let the older woman hold her, mother her until her tears ceased and it was her head that hurt instead of her heart. Wiping up her face, she sat up, ashamed to think of how she looked.

Gail gazed at her, expectantly, but also patiently. Joya wanted to say something, to respond, but there was nothing. Gail waited for several moments, then she said, "Why don't you go wash up?"

Joya nodded. She found the strength to rise and walk over to the bathroom, where she washed her face. She didn't take in her reflection, knowing she must look bad. Her eyes felt puffy, her face swollen. She sat down on the edge of the bathtub and dropped her head into her hands. She hadn't cried like that in a while. Unfortunately, she wasn't done. The tears started once again, but this time, they weren't for Michael. That was the incredulous part. She wasn't crying for her loss, or her pain. She was crying because she wanted to live again, to live fully, to love fully, to be loved, and to feel loved.

So, what was wrong with opening herself up to all that? To opening herself up to Shannon?

She thought about him. Now that she was being completely honest, she could admit there was a physical attraction there. He was a handsome man with beautiful caramel-colored skin, mixed-textured hair and strikingly good looks. More than that though, he was kind, loving and considerate. He cared for her, cared that he might have put her in a compromising situation when they started to kiss, cared enough to remain friends with her when she asked, cared enough to let go when he thought it was in her best interest. And for that, she loved him. Not just *loved* him but was *in* love with him. She understood that and now that she could admit it, she wanted it. She wanted him. Her heart was drawn to him, her soul attached to his as if he had been made for her.

So why was she holding back?

Michael.

Part of her felt she was betraying him if she loved again; but if she never let go, if she never risked her heart again, it would never be fulfilled. And never was a long time, especially if she lived to be Gail's age.

Joya sighed.

What do you have to lose? she asked herself.

Joya ceased crying, stood up and ran the hot water. She splashed it on her face, and this time, looked at herself. Not just at her reflection, but also beneath it. She wasn't as ugly as she considered earlier. No, she was beloved, and that made her beautiful.

Twenty-One

SHANNON WAS MISERABLE. HE could tolerate a good party, but not one where he was the center of attention. The open house was technically more of a marketing event, an opportunity to mingle with established and potential clients, but it was being billed around him. He was the headliner, the man of the hour, the new partner, the new name on the door. Yet, because it was all part of his new position, what he felt didn't matter. He needed to play the part expected of him.

Dressed up in a tuxedo and black tie, Shannon walked around the room, shaking hands and accepting congratulations. Some of it was heartfelt, some of it standard fare. He laughed at jokes and endured small talk with coworkers and clients. After a while, he excused himself and made his way to the makeshift bar in the back of the room. He requested a glass of champagne and loosened up his tie.

Nathan came up behind him and clapped his hand on his shoulder.

"Great turnout, Reece," he said, then motioned to the bartender to give him a glass as well.

Shannon turned around to study the room. Indeed, it was.

"It's alright," he said, tongue-in-cheek. This was Nathan's baby, his idea, his area of expertise and anything Shannon could do to rib him, he did.

"You know, this thing isn't final yet with HR," the man returned.

"Oh, is that a threat?"

"It's a promise."

"Yeah but think about how embarrassing it'll be to have to explain that to these folks here. 'Oops, just kidding. He wasn't worth it.'"

"Ah, well, when you put it that way, then I guess we'll have to let you keep the promotion. But you are most definitely worth it."

"You're not getting emotional on me, are you?"

"Me? No. Please. I'm just saying. Plus, we already printed business cards. I'd hate to have to throw those away."

The bartender slid Nathan's drink in front of him, who picked it up, held it up in a toast and took a sip. Then he leaned back against the bar to survey the room as well. The two had talked strategy before the event started, making a list of clients who needed schmoozing, and who would be doing the said-schmoozing. Marketing wasn't Shannon's strong point, but he could work a room when he needed to.

"So, where's your date?" Shannon asked him. The man had spent the better part of the day talking about the young woman he had met online whom he had invited to the open house. He usually had a couple of dates on standby, but he was really excited about this one.

"She couldn't make it," Nathan replied, with only a slight hint of disappointment in his voice. But then he smiled and said, "I see yours did though."

Shannon frowned. He hadn't invited anyone and was unsure of whom his boss was referring to. He looked at the man for clarification, but Nathan only nodded towards the front of the hall. Shannon saw clients and coworkers, but no one out of the ordinary.

Then he saw her…

Joya.

She was wearing a cream-colored, strapless gown, accentuating every curve in her body. Her beautiful brown hair hung in large curls off her shoulders and her face was done up naturally. Yes, she could make a pair of tights and a t-shirt look sexy, but never had he seen her look so gorgeous. She easily eclipsed every other woman in the room.

Then Joya locked eyes with him and

smiled. Shannon lost all thought, all ability to form a thought. His mind went blank as she started towards him, her hips swaying from side to side, bringing her closer to him. He was lost in her gaze, lost in her smile.

She stopped mere inches in front of him. Her smile never faded, but instead of saying anything to him, she turned to Nathan and warmly greeted him. Shannon continued staring, once again feeling like a teenager around her.

"You look lovely, my dear," Nathan said, then kissed her cheek.

Joya blushed.

"Thank you."

"I'm glad you could make it. Shannon here has been having a miserable time and I can't have the guest of honor looking like he'd rather be somewhere else."

At the mention of his name, Shannon snapped back to the present reality, where she had rejected him. So why was she there then?

"I'm gonna make some rounds. Don't go too far," Nathan said, leaving them alone.

"We'll be here," Joya promised, then turned back to Shannon. She tipped her head to the side, letting her curls drape across her shoulder. "Have you moved into your new office yet?" she asked him, her tone playful.

"Mostly. The personal stuff. I still have to

move my files and things," he replied. It was small talk, reminiscent of their last conversation, but until he knew why she was there, it was all he had to offer.

Joya didn't say anything else though. She only waited. Seemingly on him, her eyebrows raised slightly, as if he was supposed to say something else, something more.

Oh, yeah.

"Right. Of course. Do you want to see it?"

"Sure," she said nonchalantly, as if she hadn't been the one to bring it up.

"What about…Nathan?"

She turned around to where his boss had gone, then looked back at him.

"He'll be alright without you for a few minutes, right?" she said. Her countenance was cool, no expression visible, nothing out of place. Shannon continued gazing at her, trying to find reason in her behavior, but she gave him nothing. She only smiled at him and raised her eyebrows again, encouraging him to take her upstairs.

Shannon directed her to the elevator. There was a certain ease about her as she walked with him. She was calculated and flirty almost. Or he thought she was. He couldn't tell; and as they arrived on the tenth floor, and stepped off the elevator, Shannon decided he was done guessing. He didn't want to read into anything, especially if she had only determined they could function as friends and she was there to support him. It didn't make sense, but Shannon didn't want to get his hopes up. Not again. He needed to know.

He opened the door to his office and showed her in. There wasn't much to see: empty bookshelves, a cluttered credenza behind his desk and stacked boxes in the corner with books he had yet to unpack. The top of his desk was the only thing he had had time to organize—his laptop, an in basket, a red stapler, a magnetic knick-knack with an inspirational phrase. None of it was truly personal though, or in any way captivating. He could see that reflected on Joya's face as she walked around his office, taking everything in.

"This is quite a view," she commented stopping in front of the window.

"It's nice," he said, closing the door behind him. He walked over to the desk and leaned on the edge of it. He thought about continuing this vein of conversation, but his heart was anxious for the truth. If there was more—or less—he needed to know. "So…what are you doing here?"

Joya turned around and smiled at him again. The way she looked at him melted his heart.

"Well, I didn't have anything on my calendar and Nathan was nice enough to give me an invitation, provided I get him an invite to your mother's next party."

"Really?" he asked incredulously. He could believe the part about Nathan, but if that's all there was to it…

"No? How about I was in the neighborhood and thought I'd drop by."

Okay, so she was playing with him.

"In the neighborhood…dressed like that?"

She held her arms out, inviting him to take a better look. He did.

"It was laundry day," she replied, tongue-in-cheek.

Shannon let out a chuckle, but even as sly as she was acting, he wasn't going to let the subject go.

"Really, what are you doing here?" he asked again.

Joya's amusement turned to guilt. She dropped her arms, cleared her throat and said, "I need something from you…but I'm not sure how to ask."

Shannon's heart sank a little. This wasn't what he wanted to hear. But because his heart still yearned for her, and there was nothing he wouldn't give her, he composed himself on the inside, and with a steady tone, said,

"Name it."

In a small and hesitant voice, she said, "Kiss me?"

Shannon was unsure he heard her correctly, especially when he thought of the events of the other night. Kiss me? There weren't too many words those two could be mistaken for. *Kick* me? *Keep* me? *Keen* me? He was trying too hard now. She had said, kiss me, but it was a question, as if she was unsure he would.

Of course, he would.

If you heard her right.

What the hell was wrong with him? He heard her, but while his heart was screaming for him to act, to do as she asked, because that's all that was in him to do, it was his mind that was still in control—his level-headed, practical mind that sought to erase the doubt first.

"What?"

That was smooth.

Joya took it all in stride though, as if she had anticipated his confusion. She walked over to him, her eyes downcast and stopped in front of him. She let her body rest against the credenza before turning her gaze up to him.

"Shannon, you've been a great friend. You've given me something that's priceless in terms of love and support, and I am grateful. But it's not enough anymore. It will never be enough, and I don't think we can remain just friends."

Shannon frowned. He wasn't sure what she was trying to say. Hadn't she been the one to suggest they return to how things were between them?

"We spent all that time together," she continued, "And I would go home, missing Michael, missing what we had. I didn't understand what was happening and so I pushed you away. I denied myself the thing I wanted because I was holding onto what was—with Michael and with you. I know I'm the one who set the boundary, but I don't want that anymore."

Shannon understood then where she was going, but he still hesitated.

"What do you want?" he asked her.

Joya licked her lips, and in a small voice, said, "You."

Without waiting for him to do as she bade him, she stepped closer to him, between his outstretched legs, and closed the gap between them. Then she kissed him. Her lips were soft, tender; and as she wrapped her arms around his neck, molding her body to his, she let her desire and passion take the lead. She opened her mouth, her tongue seeking his, and kissed him with an intensity that left him breathless. All thought left him as he got lost in the moment.

Then the door behind them opened. Joya pulled away from him, her face flushed red. Shannon turned around to see Nathan, who smiled, then winked at them.

"I'd love to leave you two alone, but it's time to make your speech," the man said.

Shannon cleared his throat.

"Sure. I'll be right there."

Nathan nodded then left.

Shannon turned back to Joya, who was staring up at him with large expectant eyes. She smiled, embarrassed, then let out a sweet, melodic laugh.

"I'm sorry," he started.

She shook her head.

"I'm the one who crashed your party."

"I'm glad you did."

Then instead of leaving, he kissed her again. Short, sweet, full of desire for more.

"You…have…to…go," Joya said in between kisses.

Shannon stopped, brought his hand up to her face and gently caressed it.

"I know."

She smiled understandingly, but nonetheless stood back so he could stand and they could go. Shannon adjusted himself, trying to remove every obvious sign of what they were doing. Then he took her hand, determined not to let her go now that he had her, and together they left.

Twenty-Two

STILL BLUSHING, JOYA FOLLOWED Shannon, his hand tightly wrapped around hers. She wasn't sure why she chose this way to talk to him but after rejecting him the way she did, she knew she had to do something to make up for it. Now everything was as it should be, and they were ready to move forward. She wanted to continue what they started upstairs. However, duty was calling, and she had to relinquish Shannon for now.

They arrived downstairs. Shannon let go of her hand and joined his boss at the front of the room, turning back only briefly to look at her. Nathan garnered everyone's attention and started the program. He joked around, congratulated Shannon and then passed him the mic so that he could make a few remarks. Joya hung out in the back, but she felt as if she had a front row seat to Shannon's accomplishments. She was prouder than words could express and even if she hadn't been in love with him, she would have been honored to be there as his friend.

In love …

The idea that she could love again was still so new, but in her heart, she knew it was true.

Joya listened as Shannon thanked the firm. His eyes wandered around the room, making momentary contact with others, but when they fell on her, he lingered. His eyes brightened up and he smiled. His gaze continued moving, but Joya knew it would come back to her after a while. She anticipated it, her heart aflutter with the prospect of every contact they would make.

Shannon finished speaking. A toast was raised, and Nathan welcomed him as a partner. Then he was surrounded by clients. Shannon kept looking over to her, an apologetic expression on his face. Joya smiled understandingly, but after a few minutes, she decided she was done waiting. She strolled over to the circle of clients he was chatting with. She walked around them, catching their attention, came up behind Shannon and hooked her arm in his. All of them, including Shannon, stopped talking and watched her with rapt attention.

"Excuse me, gentleman and ladies," she said. "Mr. Reece is needed elsewhere."

No one said anything as she walked Shannon through the crowd and towards the door.

"What are you doing?" Shannon asked.

"Shh, I'm rescuing you."

He laughed.

"So if you're the boss now, you can leave your own party, right?" Joya asked him.

"Sure."

"Well, come on then," she insisted. They arrived at the elevator. Joya pressed the button to recall it to their floor. When the doors opened, she stepped inside and beckoned him to follow. He did without hesitation.

"Where are we going?" Shannon asked.

Joya didn't need to think it over. She knew what she wanted, and though she had never been the forward type, she was ready to embrace whatever the evening held. Even if it required a little steering.

"Well, I haven't had dinner yet," she said coyly, though it wasn't a lie. She had been so nervous about seeing Shannon, she forgot to eat.

"Where do you want to go?"

"Back to your place? Get something homecooked? Then do a little dessert?" she said, her tone suggestive.

Shannon only gazed at her though, his eyebrows arched.

"Are you sure?" he eventually asked. It seemed his mind was in the same place as hers.

Joya smiled, then leaned over, rose up on her toes and kissed him.

"Yes," she said.

Without another word, Shannon took her hand in his, and together they exited the elevator, and walked to the parking deck, where his car was located. He opened the door for her and helped her inside. Then she waited with bated breath for him to join her. Shannon started the car, but before he drove off, he turned to her and asked, "So why the change of heart?"

Joya understood that he wanted to be sure. She was the one who initially said 'no', after all.

"Gail," Joya responded. "We had a heart-to-heart and she reminded me I had more living to do."

Shannon chuckled.

"What?"

"She and Ma were in cahoots."

"What do you mean?"

"Ma told me she was trying to set us up."

Joya raised an eyebrow but conceded, "They did a good job."

"Don't tell them that—it'll only encourage them. Next they'll be trying to get grandkids."

Joya smiled at the thought but didn't say anything. All of that would come with time.

THERE WASN'T much conversation as they drove to Shannon's place. When they arrived, he gave her a quick tour. It was larger than her apartment, with a modern appearance. He showed her around the living room, through the kitchen and by the bedroom. After spending a majority of the summer at his mother's home, it lacked the country hospitality she had become accustomed to. Still, because it was his home, there was an appeal to it.

Shannon undid his tie and pulled it off.

"You can get comfortable if you want," Joya said, not wanting to restrict him simply because she was overdressed for the occasion. She didn't plan to end the evening that way anyway.

"What about you? I don't have anything for you to wear."

"I'm sure I can find something."

She walked into his closet and went through it. Shannon followed her and leaned on the doorframe to watch her. She held out a basic blue button-down shirt.

"That's not really comfortable," he advised.

She hung the shirt back up and pulled out a jersey.

"What about this?" she asked.

Shannon opened his mouth to respond but didn't. Then he hesitated a moment too long.

"I know I said 'whatsoever', but I may

have to draw the line there. It's signed."

Joya laughed and picked a t-shirt. It was bigger than anything she normally wore, but she didn't figure on wearing it long. It had been a while since she seduced anyone, but she knew she didn't start off by prancing around the house naked. She had to work her way to that…though she didn't think Shannon would mind either way.

Shannon drew in a breath of anticipation, and said, "I'll be in the kitchen."

She kicked off her shoes and unzipped her dress. She stepped out of it and laid it down on a nearby chair. Wearing only a strapless bra and matching panties, she pulled the t-shirt over her head and readjusted her hair. She preferred it pulled back in a ponytail, but she liked the way she looked and wanted to keep the mood going.

Joya walked back to the kitchen, where Shannon had pulled out a variety of food items. He had taken off his jacket and removed his button down, leaving only the white t-shirt he had worn beneath it. He never looked as sexy as he did now.

Joya cleared her throat to get his attention. Shannon looked up at her, his expression stunned as she placed her hands on her hips and modeled the t-shirt for him.

"You look better in that than I ever did,"

he said.

She smiled and joined him at the counter. Together, they prepared some basic chicken wraps and a salad. The ambience was relaxed as they sat at the counter and ate, their conversation light, their gaze focused on each other. They eventually moved to the couch, where Joya relaxed into Shannon's embrace. He wrapped his arms around her and held her, devotedly, protectively, lovingly. There was nothing exciting about the moment, nothing awe-inspiring or amazing. It was quiet, intimate, love; and before they kissed again, it was all Joya needed.

Twenty-Three

SHANNON HAD BEEN AWAKE FOR a while now. He tried falling back to sleep, but his heart was so full, it felt as if it might explode. Instead he rolled over and watched Joya sleep. Her body was turned away from him, her hair spread out on her back and shoulders, covering her like a blanket, still looking as radiant as she did when she crashed his party. Part of him couldn't believe this was real. After spending the evening with her though, after making love to her, falling asleep in each other's arms and waking up and seeing her there with him, Shannon had no doubt. The night, their relationship, their future, them—it was all real.

Joya stirred in her sleep, rolling over onto her other side so that she was facing him. Shannon didn't move but continued watching her. When she settled next to him, he waited a moment, then let his hand rest on her shoulder. He ran his hand down her arm, his touch gentle, light. He didn't want to wake her, he simply wanted to feel her body beneath his hand, to feel the warmth of her skin next to his. He stopped when he reached her back, and left his hand there, watching it rise and fall with every breath she took.

"Don't stop," Joya said softly. Her eyes were closed, but there was a small smile on her face. Shannon resumed his gentle caress, until she opened them and met his gaze. She rolled over onto her side, her eyes still on him.

"I love you," she said, her voice soft, content.

"I love you," he replied, and took her in a tender kiss. She pulled him close to her and responded in kind, inviting him into her mouth and into her warmth. Shannon made love to her, savoring every touch between them. And when their passion had culminated, Shannon simply held her, unwilling to let her go, unwilling to forget this moment, especially now that he knew what it felt like to be loved by the one his heart belonged to.

DAY BROKE, and Shannon woke up with Joya still in his arms. They were slow to start their day, enjoying each other's company, enjoying each other's embrace. This was something new for both of them and they were relishing every moment, every promise of what was ahead of them. Eventually though, they got up and got ready. Joya put her gown back on while Shannon dressed a little less formal, wearing a pair of khakis and a polo. Everything was perfect.

Then his phone rang. Shannon groaned—he didn't want the interruption. They were dressed though and ready to face the day. He answered his phone while Joya checked the messages on hers.

"Jackie, Jackie…"

It was his mother, but her voice was trembling, panicking.

"Ma, what is it?"

He turned to Joya, whose face had crestfallen as she listened to her voicemails.

"I left a message for Joya, but she didn't answer."

"What's wrong?"

"It's Gail…," she explained. Her words followed in a rush: the woman had been taken to the hospital after a neighbor found her unresponsive and foaming at the mouth. They thought it might be a heart attack but wouldn't know until they got to the hospital.

"If only I had been there…," Joya lamented as they drove to his mother's house before heading over to the hospital.

"Don't do that," he told her. "It's not your fault."

She didn't listen though, only repeated the same words.

If only she had been there with her …

If only she had stayed …

If only she had gone home …

Shannon wanted to believe she didn't regret spending the night with him, but he also couldn't get the thought out of his mind that maybe he was as guilty as Joya felt. He was the one who took her home with him. If he had been anything of a gentleman, if he wasn't so selfish, if he had taken her home instead, perhaps Gail wouldn't have been alone. Or she might have gotten help sooner. Instead, his auntie was in the hospital and he was worried about his relationship with Joya.

Shannon stopped at his mother's place long enough to pick her up, then they drove to the hospital. He helped her out of the car while Joya went inside and tried to get information on Gail. There was none yet, leaving them in limbo. They took a seat in the lobby and waited. Shannon sat between both women. He squeezed his mom's hand but took hold of Joya's and held it tightly to his chest to let her know he was there for her. He didn't think she was aware of his presence though. She was instead focused on the likelihood that Gail was going to die. Having lost Michael after giving up her own family, Shannon wasn't sure Joya could face that prospect and return to life unscathed. He knew she would survive, but he wasn't sure she did.

Minutes turned into hours, leaving them all anxious. He was becoming fidgety himself, when a middle-aged female doctor joined them in the waiting room.

"Are you Gail Evans' family?"

"Yes," he said.

She encouraged them to sit back down and joined them.

"I'm Dr. Huang, Gail's oncologist. She's resting now, but—"

Evelyn interrupted.

"Oncologist?"

The woman nodded.

"Gail has lymphoma cancer."

Joya's tears flowed now.

"What?" she exclaimed.

"It's in the early stages," the doctor continued, her voice calm. "*If* she starts chemotherapy right away, she's got a good chance at survival—"

"What do you mean, *if...*?" Joya interrupted.

Dr. Huang shook her head.

"She has refused treatment."

"Is she even in the right frame of mind to make that decision now?" Joya injected.

"Actually, she came to me a couple of months back after her doctor referred her to me. I diagnosed her and was ready to start a treatment plan, but she said no."

"Why would Gail say no?" Evelyn demanded.

"Everyone reacts differently when faced with news like this. For some, it's a death sentence. They don't see any point in even trying. For others, it's a signal to fight. Gail is probably somewhere near the former. I understand her husband died from cancer as well. That likely has a bearing on her decision. She may not want to relive that experience. In any case, while this is bad news, she still has a good chance of survival, but we have to start treatment immediately."

The doctor stopped, as if she understood they were going to need time to process everything she shared. Shannon felt like a ton of bricks had been dropped on him. And as strong as he wanted to be for his mother, and Joya especially, he felt helpless.

"Can we see her now?" he asked.

"We're getting a room for her. We'll come get you when it's ready."

Dr. Huang excused herself. Joya leaned back into the chair behind her, a lost expression on her face. Evelyn stood up and sat down in the seat on the opposite side of Joya. She placed her uncasted arm around her and held her.

"She's going to quit," Joya lamented. "She's just going to quit."

"She's sick. She's not thinking right," Evelyn said. "We'll talk to her."

Joya shook her head.

"No, that's why she pushed me to go after Shannon. She wanted to make sure I wasn't left alone when she died."

Evelyn turned her gaze up to Shannon. He understood then she and Gail might have been in cahoots regarding the matchmaking, but it seemed even his mother was kept in the dark about the woman's true motives.

The three of them waited for a nurse to come get them. There were no words between them, only impatient sighs. Eventually Joya stood up to go to the restroom. Evelyn offered to go with her, but Joya only shook her head and left.

Evelyn sat back in her chair, her expression mirroring what he was feeling. Despite their relationship with Gail, both of them seemed to understand that the loss would hit Joya harder.

Without looking at him, Evelyn said, "I'm going to eventually die too."

Shannon knew it was the situation that had her talking like that.

"You're too ornery to die," he responded, hoping to lighten the mood.

She wasn't going to let it go though. She touched his arm and said, "Look at me,

Junior Shannon Reece."

She never called him by his given name, unless he was in trouble and though he had stopped sweating the nervousness that followed her use of his name, he did look at her, his heart beating hard.

"I know I act like I'm invincible sometimes," she said holding up her cast. "And we want to believe those we love will be around forever, but I'm not going to be here much longer, and I want you to be ready."

"I know, Ma," he said. He really did. The prospect of her death was a niggling thought when he hit thirty and she was fifty-five. Now that he was the one who was fifty, Shannon had no choice but to come to terms with the fact that his mother wouldn't be with him much longer. Yes, she could very well live to be a hundred, but she could also die soon. Nothing in life was a given. "I know," he repeated. More so for himself, because now the situation was reversed: he was older than Joya. He would die before she did. Could he ask her to love him? He'd only end up hurting her.

Twenty-Four

JOYA TRIED TO GET COMFORTABLE on the couch in Gail's room, but the chair was hard. She was also still wearing the gown she had worn to the party yesterday. It was evening, and Shannon had gone to her apartment to get her a change of clothes after taking Evelyn home. The older woman had grown tired sitting in the hospital all day. Shannon hesitated to leave Joya alone, but she insisted she would be alright until he returned.

At least she hoped she would be. Joya was touched by the thought that Gail was looking out for her in her matchmaking schemes, but she wasn't ready to give up the older woman. Maybe it was selfish of her, maybe she was thinking only of herself, but she needed Gail in her life. Once upon a time, she was her only tie to Michael, but now she was more than that. Joya had grown to love her and view her as she did her own mother.

Gail stirred, turning her head from one side to the other, but she remained asleep.

Joya had talked further with Dr. Huang when she returned to check on Gail earlier. The woman was patient with Joya, answering all her questions about the cancer and Gail's prospective treatment should they convince her to agree to it. Even with everything Gail had been through, Joya had to believe the woman still had something else to live for…though her own positivity was ebbing away.

Gail moved again, this time, opening her eyes. She looked about her, confused by her surroundings. Joya stood up and approached the bed.

"Gail?"

The older woman looked at her, then smiled.

"How are you?" Joya asked.

"Alright, baby," Gail said as she closed her eyes, still sleepy. She took a deep breath and opened them again. "How did the party go?"

"Fine," Joya replied. It was all she could say without breaking down.

"Did you talk to Shannon?" Gail asked her.

Joya nodded.

"And?"

The tears escaped once again, silencing her voice. She managed a smile but was unable to muster up the strength to talk about her and Shannon. Especially when there were more pressing matters at hand, matters of life and death, matters Gail seemed hell-bent on ignoring.

"He's a good man," Gail said. "He'll take

care of you and make you happy, you'll see."

Joya couldn't hold her tongue anymore.

"Why didn't you tell me?" she asked.

"I didn't want you upset," Gail said point blankly.

"Is it true you don't want treatment?"

Gail took in another deep breath and in a calm voice, explained, "Joya, I'm old. I've lived my life. I loved a wonderful man, had a son I was proud of. I'm ready to go."

"What good is life without you?"

"You have Shannon. You won't be alone."

"It's not that simple."

"Joya, you were a wonderful wife to my son, but he's gone. Earnest is gone. They're all gone and soon it'll be my turn. I don't want to postpone the inevitable. I'm ready to go."

"But Dr. Huang said the cancer is still in its early stages. You have a lot of good years ahead of you if you start treatment."

Gail wouldn't listen though.

"You'll understand when you get to be where I'm at," she said coldly, then closed her eyes and turned her head to the side, ready to sleep again. Or end the conversation. Joya sat on the edge of the bed and touched Gail's hand. The woman didn't turn to her though. Joya let the tears fall.

SHANNON RETURNED after a while. He didn't ask her any questions, only handed her the bag he had packed for her.

"I'll be right here," he assured her.

She offered him a small smile and went to the bathroom to change. She rummaged through the bag and found a pair of jeans and a t-shirt. There was also a small toiletry bag that he purchased on the way back to the hospital. She smiled in appreciation at his thoughtfulness. She needed that right now.

Joya washed up and changed. Then she repacked her dress and exited the bathroom. She dropped the bag on the floor next to the door and went to join Shannon on the couch, but he had chosen to sit in the solitary chair, opposite the bed. He was leaning forward, elbows on his knees, as if bearing the weight of the world on his shoulders. While she was certain of the love he had for her, there was something about his stance that was off-putting—he was closing her off.

Joya brushed off the thought. She was being selfish. Gail had been a part of his life longer than she had been hers. He was allowed to grieve and hurt anyway he needed to. Though she really wanted to sit with him, to hold him, to share in that pain, she slid past him and sat back down on the couch. She lifted her leg up and wrapped her arm around it, holding it close to her.

"How's she doing?" he finally asked.

"She's ready to die." The words were bitter in Joya's mouth. "Michael's death hit her harder than I thought."

Shannon sat back in his chair and made eye contact with her. His gaze was distant, empty though.

"Am I being selfish for wanting her to live?" Joya asked, seeking some kind of comfort from him. "I don't know what I'll do if she dies," she admitted.

"I think we're all selfish when it comes to the people we love," he said. It was more of a general statement than an assurance. Joya reminded herself to be patient—perhaps it was all he had to give. Indeed, Shannon looked back down, his eyes on the floor in front of him and said nothing else.

Joya felt alone.

DR. HUANG made the decision to keep Gail another day for observation. Joya was ready to stay with her, but Shannon insisted on taking her home to rest.

"I don't think I can go back to the apartment," Joya told him.

"You can stay with Ma."

Joya had hoped he would want her to stay with him, but she didn't argue. She kissed

Gail goodnight, grabbed her bag and prepared to go. Ever the gentleman, Shannon insisted on carrying the bag for her. She let him. He took her to get her car, then followed her back to Evelyn's place. She was still up when they arrived at her house. The older woman hugged her and treated her as she would a daughter, reminding her of Gail.

Joya joined Evelyn at the kitchen table, while Shannon leaned back against the counter. He was nearby but still distant. She was going to have to talk to him. Right now, though, she needed to focus on Gail. Joya updated Evelyn on her condition but couldn't offer any of her usual cheerful disposition. It wasn't in her tonight.

"I should have seen this," she bemoaned. "I should have known she was fading away."

"Don't do that, Joya," Evelyn corrected her. "It's not your fault. Gail has always been like that—didn't say much, but she felt it deeply. She just needs to work through this."

"Yeah, but I watched her bury Michael. I knew she was depressed. I should have paid more attention."

"We're not going to see everything, no matter how much we try."

"So, what then? We let her die?"

"No, I didn't say that. We just can't take on the responsibility of her decision.

Ultimately, her fate is in her hands," Evelyn said. "What we can do is help her focus on what she's got left to live for. After my Jack died, there were days I would have gladly gone with him. He was my life, my breath; and I couldn't fathom life without him, but I had to remember I had Jackie. I would have surely given up if I didn't have him." She looked up at Shannon, a loving gleam in her eye, then turned back to Joya. "Gail's lost much, but she's also forgotten what she has and that's what we need to help her see so she can make the best decision possible for her. We need to remind her of what she still has."

Evelyn paused, an expression of sudden realization moving over her face. She looked up at Shannon again, who apparently understood what was going on with his mother. He bore a thoughtful, almost amused look on his face. Joya wasn't sure what they were communicating in their silence.

"What?" she asked.

Shannon nodded his approval, then said, "We throw a party."

Joya frowned. This seemed to be Evelyn's answer to everything, and right now, Joya didn't understand how a party could solve anything.

Or how Shannon could agree to it.

Evelyn must have seen the confused look

on her face, because she patted Joya's hand and explained.

"Big John, God bless him, he and I didn't always get along, but one thing he taught me was to appreciate the people we love while they are still living. Don't wait until they've passed, he told us, but let them know now how they impacted our lives, how much we love them and need them. Birthdays were always big occasions, as were holidays. I was a scrawny little colored girl who thought she knew it all, but he taught me a thing or two about that. Even while the man was dying, he made sure we did the same for him, what you would call a living funeral today. Jackie, you remember that?"

Shannon chuckled.

"Yeah. All the family gathered at the farm. Uncle Liam brought a wood coffin with him, decorated it, even got in it. Gave me nightmares for weeks."

Evelyn laughed.

"I had forgotten about that."

"Pa didn't find it so funny, but Granddad loved it."

Joya watched as they reminisced about the party. She recalled then what Shannon had shared with her about memories. She had been so focused on Michael's death, it was all she remembered. Maybe if she helped Gail recall life, the same way Shannon helped her, she could help her heal, in more than one way.

"Let's do that," Joya said suddenly, interrupting Evelyn. She would never be so purposely rude, but where she was hopeless before, she knew in her heart this was the route they needed to take. "Let's throw a party for her. I'll call the family, get everything set up and we'll remind her about the good things she's got left."

Evelyn laughed again.

"Slow down, baby. You know I love a good party, but you have to go into this knowing we can't make her change her mind."

"I know," Joya said. She wasn't sure she did, but she said it anyway, hoping to convince Evelyn. "We have to try though."

"Alright then. Let's start planning."

Twenty-Five

SHANNON RETURNED TO HIS home late that evening. He should have been glad to be there, but it was filled with memories of Joya. He started to recall their evening together but decided to put the thoughts away. No matter how precious they were to him, none of them would help him do what he needed to do.

Though it was late, Shannon called Nathan to apprise him of the situation. As always, the man was understanding and told him to take as much time as he needed. Shannon knew he wouldn't always be able to do this every time something happened to his mother, or Gail, or any other elderly family member, but having earned the time after the long years and many hours he gave to the firm, Shannon decided to take it. He'd resolve whatever he could, then go back.

Back to what though? His job? His position? His life? How much was it worth without Joya? He had only spent one night with her, but she had made such an impact on his life. He would never be the same.

If you truly love her, you'll let her go.

Regardless of the impression she left on him though, he had to put distance between them. Beginning now. The conversation would eventually come up, but if he let her go now, it would be easier later.

That's what he wanted to believe anyway.

In the morning, he picked Joya and Evelyn up and went to the hospital. Dr. Huang was there and while her recommendation was still for treatment, she advised them about the course of the disease, and what to expect. They might have dismissed the whole thing before as a bad dream, but there was no denying it now. This was the reality they were facing.

Gail, for her part, remained stoic. She had made her decision and she would not be moved. Shannon's heart hurt to see her so indifferent, but it was her choice.

Dr. Huang discharged her, and Shannon got his car. Everyone was quiet as they left. They went to Joya and Gail's apartment; and while his mother and Joya got settled in, he hung out in the background. Gail didn't want the attention, but after the health scare, she didn't have a leg to stand on. They fussed over her and made sure she was comfortable, and when she had gone to sleep, they talked about the party. Joya made lists while Evelyn spouted out ideas about what type of music they should play, what kind of food they should serve and what family needed to be contacted. Shannon listened as the two of them made preparations.

"Where do we want to do this?" Joya asked.

Evelyn sat back, a smug look on her face.

"Well, I'd say my place. I mean the house has had some repairs, it's looking good, clean and clear of boxes and clutter, but I guess it's not my house anymore."

Shannon rolled his eyes. Could she be any more obvious?

"I'm just saying," she continued, "It's a large house, with several acres and it was like a second home to Gail for many years. It's familiar and tried."

Joya smiled at Evelyn's lack of subtlety.

"And if it were still mine, I wouldn't charge you for the venue."

Shannon shook his head incredulously as Joya let out a chuckle.

"Fine, Ma," he said. "We'll have the party there, but you're moving afterward."

"We'll see," she replied and returned to the planning. Shannon let the subject drop—it wasn't something he wanted to discuss now, because if she was pushing for the house, then it wouldn't be too long before she was asking about him and Joya. She had eyes and he knew she could see the change in their relationship. She didn't say anything though, which had Shannon worried. What was she planning now?

Back at the house, Shannon helped his mother to her room, said goodnight and went upstairs to his former room. He could have gone to his home but found it easier not to.

For the next two weeks, this was his routine. He ran errands and helped prep the house for the guests. When he wasn't doing that, he was shuttling his mother to Joya's place, so she could spend time with her friend. Joya continued helping Gail and preparing for the party. He limited his words to her, making sure his mom was there to continue the discussion. He wasn't one to *ghost* anyone, in apparently what was a common way to break things off nowadays, but with everything that was happening, he couldn't bring himself to initiate the conversation. Apparently, she couldn't either, as she never asked, never pushed for an explanation, just kept their relationship platonic.

Perhaps the whole affair was fleeting after all.

They adjusted to their new normal and with a date set for the party, Shannon opted to go back to work. He had begun transitioning to his new responsibilities months earlier, so the workload wasn't very different. This was simply the first time that summer he was able to focus completely on work. It was a welcome distraction. He cleaned up his new office, put away his files and was working on his emails when his assistant knocked on the door.

"Come in," he said.

She opened the door and stuck her head in.

"You have a guest." And without waiting for him, she opened the door and stepped to the side. Joya stood behind her. She was dressed in capris and a sleeveless blouse, her hair up in a ponytail, her make-up simple and radiant, just like her smile. Shannon got excited to see her, then remembered why he couldn't be. The secretary showed her in, then shut the door behind her as she exited.

"What are you doing here?" he asked Joya.

"I was in the neighborhood and decided to stop by and see you."

She wandered over to the window, nonchalantly, as if she belonged there; and given the space she occupied in his heart, she most certainly did. However, her visit only served to guilt Shannon further. He should have talked to her sooner, should have explained why they couldn't be together. At the very least, he owed her that.

"Listen, Joya…," he began, but the rest

of the explanation jammed in his throat when Joya turned away from the window, walked over to his desk and leaned against it, filling his brain with the memories of their last encounter, there and at home.

"You've been ignoring me," she said, meeting his gaze.

"I wanted to give you space," he said, quickly.

"Gail was your family first."

"She was Michael's mom and I know you two have a special relationship."

Joya didn't look convinced though.

"What happened?" she asked. "One minute, you and I were fine; then everything occurred with Gail, and you've been distant ever since. What happened?"

Shannon saw the hurt in her eyes and struggled to find the right words. How could he adequately explain what even his heart was fighting against?

"I don't regret you and me," she continued. "I don't regret being with you. I love you. I'm *in love* with you. I meant it when I said it then and I mean it now."

Shannon sighed.

"And I love you," he admitted.

"So, what's going on?" she pleaded.

"Joya, is that enough?"

"Isn't it?" she demanded.

"I'm older than you."

"And?"

"I'm not too far behind Ma and Ms. Gail; and they already have one foot in the grave. What am I offering you besides heartache if I pass? *When* I pass?"

"Love. Friendship. Companionship."

She wasn't making this easy for him.

"For how long though?" he asked. "One day, probably sooner than later, that will be me lying on that hospital bed, breaking your heart. I can't ask you to do that for me."

Joya moved closer to him. Closer than they had been these past two weeks. Shannon wasn't sure he would be able to resist any longer if she continued invading his space.

"Michael was younger than you and he's gone. The possibility that you will outlive me is just as real as the one where I outlive you. Shannon, there are no guarantees—in love, in life, in anything. I thought I'd have forever with Michael, and only we got six years. If I got half of that with you, it'd be enough because I love you. Or is that not enough for you?" Joya was more worked up now than he had seen her in the last couple of months. Even if he wanted to reply, he couldn't. She continued talking, determined to make him see her point. "Are you willing to pass up the chance to love, and to be loved, just because of a few years between us? I'm not. If life has taught me nothing else, it's that it's far too precious to wait around. If we do that, then it'll be gone too soon. So…" Joya took a deep breath and calmed down. She dropped to one knee and met his gaze. Shannon didn't want to think about the implication of her actions. He just waited with bated breath. "I have a request for you, and you said whatsoever I desired, you would give me."

She stared at him, expectantly, as if waiting for him to ask.

"What do you desire?" he inquired, hesitantly.

"Marry me."

Shannon knew he had heard her, knew he knew the words she spoke. No different than when she asked him to kiss her. But now, like then, he had a problem registering the words. Did she mean for *him* to marry her? For him to be her husband and her to be his wife?

God, why was this so hard? He wanted Joya, wanted to be with her, yet part of him was still fighting it.

"Are you sure?" he asked.

"Yes." There was no hesitation in her voice. "I don't know how it was with your previous relationships, but I'm not letting you go so easy. And besides that, I'm not done writing the story of my life. If this is truly going to be the Book of Joy, then there has to be some joy in it. So, what do you say? Are you going to marry me?"

Shannon could no longer resist or object. She was right, about the situation and about him especially. He had made a habit of pushing others away, but no other woman had fought as hard to keep him either. If she wasn't letting him go, then neither was he letting her go.

"Yes," he said. "Yes, I'll marry you."

"Good," she said, then cupped his face and kissed him. She didn't wait for an invitation, didn't wait for him to react, just kissed him, deeply, passionately, lovingly, making up for the time they spent apart.

"I love you," he told her, as she pulled away.

She stared into his eyes, a mischievous smile on her face.

"And I love you, Junior Shannon Reece."

And as much as Shannon didn't like to hear his name out loud, he had to admit there was a certain appeal to it when Joya said it.

Twenty-Six

GAIL CLIMBED BACK INTO BED after using the restroom and lay down. She felt better than she had the past couple of weeks, but she was still weak, still tired. The pain was intermittent, but manageable. Dr. Huang had talked to her about treatment and let her know what she should expect. She had even suggested counseling, but Gail was confident in her decision. And now that Joya was getting remarried, she could truly rest. Gail never imagined everything working out as quickly as it did, but she was glad, for Joya's sake— and hers.

Gail stayed in bed most of the day. She and Joya were going to Evelyn's house later that evening to celebrate the removal of Evelyn's cast. It wouldn't be the big to-do she usually planned, but something intimate for the four of them. Gail wouldn't call it a final hurrah, but she understood this was just a glimpse of changes to come. No wedding date was set, but Joya would be moving out soon. Evelyn's living situation was still not resolved (from her perspective, anyway), but she too would most likely be moving in with Shannon. Only Gail would remain where she was—in her apartment and in her life.

When early afternoon came, Gail rose and showered up. She took her time getting ready and was feeling good when Joya finally got home from work.

"You look wore out," she commented as Joya walked in and dropped onto the couch. It was rare that the woman was not smiling, but even now, as tired as she was, her face was lit up.

"I don't know where they get all that energy," she sighed and ran her hand over her face. The diamond ring on her left hand caught the light and sparkled. It had been Evelyn's ring; the one Jack gave her over fifty years earlier. The woman insisted when Shannon announced their engagement and while the gesture was sweet, all Gail could see was that the transference was complete. Joya would no longer be Michael's wife and Gail would no longer be her mother-in-law.

"You just need to get back into the swing of things," Gail encouraged her.

"I know," Joya said, then got up. "Well, let me wash up and we can go," she said and left for the bathroom. She was ready within thirty minutes and came out into the living room, looking refreshed. "You ready?"

Gail nodded and stood up. Pain shot through her body and she grasped the side of the couch to steady her. Joya reached out to help Gail. The pain passed, but it didn't change the expression of concern on her daughter-in-law's face. Despite the discomfort in her body, Gail stood up straight, and said, "I'm fine."

"You're not," Joya said, sadly. "You're sick."

Gail shook her head and gently patted Joya on her hand.

"I'm fine," she insisted and before the woman could argue, she started towards the door. She didn't like walking away from her daughter-in-law, but she wasn't in the mood to argue about it now.

Joya came up behind her and took her by the arm. She didn't say anything though, only walked with her to the car. She helped her in and then drove to Evelyn's house without saying much. Oh, she talked about the little kids in her class, about seeing Hannah in the hallway, about her lessons and about school, but she didn't say anything else about Gail's health.

When they arrived at Evelyn's house, Joya helped her out and walked her to the front porch, which had been fixed following the Independence Day party.

"Why are we using this door?"

"Shannon is replacing the back steps."

Gail nodded and followed her daughter-in-law onto the porch. Joya knocked and opened the door. Then she stepped aside so Gail could enter. She was ready to announce herself but was stunned to find a crowd of people inside the house, smiling, and yelling, "Surprise!"

And not just anyone, but familiar faces. Certainly, the Reece's, who had treated her like family for many years, but also her own family. Cousins, nieces, nephews, and grands. Even her sister Myrna was there. She was the first to come up to her and hug her.

"What are you doing here?" Gail asked.

Myrna let her go and stared at her incredulously, as if the answer was obvious.

"For you, of course," she said, matter-of-factly. She stepped back and allowed others to come forward to greet and hug her. One after another, until Gail lost count. She was overwhelmed with emotion and for a moment wanted to pull away from everyone to compose herself. This was when she saw Evelyn and Shannon.

"Hey Auntie," Shannon said, and kissed her cheek.

"What's all this?" she asked.

"We're celebrating you, silly," Evelyn said. "We weren't going to wait until you were gone to let you know how much we love you. Come on."

They walked into the living room, where she took a seat in the recliner. Drinks and food were passed out, as music and conversations filled the air. Family members continued flocking to her, hugging and kissing her. Though the visits were brief, their messages of love had her crying. She brushed the tears away as quickly as she could but found the whole exercise to be futile. They weren't going to stop. Her heart felt heavy. No, it was full; with the love everyone was showing her, but also with the knowledge that her friend had set this up. Evelyn was nothing if not the true definition of friendship.

"You are crazy," Gail said to Evelyn, who had made her way to the seat beside her. She had to raise her voice so that Evelyn could hear her over the crowd.

"Me?"

"For doing all this."

Evelyn shook her head.

"Not this time. This is all Joya."

Gail frowned in disbelief.

"I know, right?" Evelyn stated. "Parties are usually my thing, but Joya was the mastermind this time. And I'll tell you what, that girl was determined. She almost single-handedly put this party together."

She nodded towards the kitchen. Gail

turned to see Joya and Shannon approaching them, a cup in each hand. Joya handed one to Gail and one to Evelyn.

"You did this?" Gail asked her.

Joya nodded.

"You didn't have to."

"I wanted to."

She smiled, almost deviously, and turned to Shannon, who gave her a cup. She yelled for silence, but everyone continued talking. Shannon let out a loud whistle that garnered everyone's attention and then pointed proudly to Joya.

"Thank you for coming everyone. I just want to say a few words and then you can go back to the party. We all know Gail in one way or another. I met her several months into dating Michael. I was nervous, but he kept assuring me his mom would love me. And indeed, she did. She was the sweetest, most beautiful woman I had met. She had a quiet strength that I wanted to emulate, especially after my own mom asked me to make a choice between the family I had grown up with and the family I now wanted as my own. And when I made that choice, Gail was there with open arms. And has been ever since. We might not share the same blood, but she is my mother nonetheless and I wanted to publicly thank her for making me feel loved."

Joya looked at her, her eyes wet with unshed tears. She leaned down towards her and in a more personable voice, added, "I love you, Mom. That's what you are and regardless of how long we have left together, that's what you will always be to me." She turned back to the crowd and raised her cup. "To Mom."

Others joined in on the toast.

Gail felt shame now. She had never looked at Joya as more than her daughter-*in-law*. Certainly, she loved her and felt fortunate to have someone like her in her life, but at the end of the day, she was nothing more than that.

The music resumed.

Joya knelt beside Gail, who immediately cupped her face in her hand and gazed at her, as if seeing her for the first time. No words were necessary. Joya seemed to understand. Gail released her and pulled her daughter-in-law—nay, her daughter—in for a hug. They held onto each other for what seemed a long time, before Gail eventually let go.

"Did you need anything else?" Joya asked her.

"No, baby."

Joya kissed her and stood up. She turned to Shannon and the two disappeared into the crowd.

For the next hour, Gail kept busy, catching up with the other family members. There weren't too many questions about her health, but more than once, she heard about how sweet Joya was, how lucky Gail was to have her, how even though she lost Michael, she still had Joya. Gail knew she was lucky. No, she was blessed. She hadn't seen it before, but she did now, and she wanted more than anything else to make up for it.

"Michael found himself a good thing when he married Joya."

Evelyn's voice broke her out of her thoughts. Gail looked over to her friend, who had returned to her chair after playing the role of the good hostess for a while.

"He did an even better thing when he gave her to you as a daughter." She gazed at Gail straight on, her tone colored with sorrow. "I know she was Michael's first, but Shannon will be good to her."

She pointed over to the doorway, beyond the crowd, where the happy couple were standing close to each other, her arms wrapped around his neck, barely any air between them. Joya's heart was mending, which meant Gail's could as well…if she let it.

"I know I can't take the place of Earnest and Michael," Evelyn continued, "And I would never try. Despite my arrogance and immaturity sometimes, I do understand you just can't replace the loved ones you lose. But I need you. *We* need you. And you need us. We're family."

Gail let the tears fall anew. She didn't even try to hide them anymore.

If I let it… she had convinced herself she was ready to go, but she wasn't so sure now.

"So, stick around with me, okay? We'll take care of each other. Plus, you know that Shannon is fifty and Joya has been waiting for a baby for a while now. If we hold out one year, we'll be holding our first grandchild," she said motioning again towards Shannon and Joya, who were now kissing. "Maybe even sooner," Evelyn added, matter-of-factly.

Gail couldn't help but chuckle at her commentary.

"What do you say? You gonna stick around? Will you start treatment?"

The prospect of losing anyone else scared her. She missed Earnest and Michael and all the others who had gone before them, but the thought of missing what was to come scared her even more.

"Okay, give me something to work with here. I've never been good at this sort of thing. And the truth is, I told Joya that we had to go into this knowing you might not change your mind. But I'm not good at that either. So, what do you say?"

Gail looked over to Evelyn, whose eyes were filled with the uncertainty everyone was feeling these days. Uncertainty, but also all the love she had for her, love that surpassed everything else and still called to her, even when she had given up—something Gail had done a long time ago.

If I let it … Gail couldn't control what would happen, but it didn't mean she couldn't make the most of it.

"Gail?"

"Yes, yes, yes," she finally said, her voice hoarse and choking with tears.

Evelyn grasped her hand and squeezed it, tears now flowing down her face. She pulled Gail towards her and hugged her. Gail let her love envelope her.

After a minute, Evelyn released her and with sudden confidence, said, "Okay, good. Because now that Shannon and Joya are together, we've got to figure out how I'm going to keep my house. I've got some ideas, but I'm going to need your help …"

Gail smiled. The woman was nothing if not persistent. Perhaps this was why, despite their lack of professional matchmaking skills, they succeeded in getting their kids together. So maybe Evelyn would find a way to convince Shannon to keep the house. It would likely be a hair-brained and crazy idea. Gail suddenly had a desire to see it through. Not just that either, but also Shannon and Joya's wedding. And their first child. And possibly their second. And everything else life had for them, good or bad. Gail was looking forward to seeing it all.

Read on for the first chapter of

STAY WITH ME

Runner-up
2016 Shelf Unbound Best Indie Book

Noah is stocking shelves at the local bookstore when Alma walks in and kisses him. He has barely enough time to grasp what's happening when she ends the kiss and walks away. Too intrigued not to respond, the normally introverted shopkeeper goes after Alma...only to discover keeping up with the outgoing vixen is more difficult than he imagined.

Everything Alma does is impulsive, and Noah is no different. The good-looking, but reserved clerk captured her attention on a previous visit and since then she's been determined to steal a kiss. However, seeing him again after the purloined smooch was not part of her plan; and now that he wants to get to know her, Alma finds the future she's carefully planned is suddenly uncertain.

With the odds stacked against them, Noah and Alma must decide if their fledgling relationship is worth pursuing, because if they can get past their doubts and insecurities, they might just have a future together.

One

THE CHIME ON THE DOOR announced the arrival of a customer to Mister Bill's Used Books. Noah could hear it from the stockroom. He thought nothing of it though and continued unpacking the box in front of him. Mister Bill, or rather just Bill, stocked mostly used books, donated from libraries, customers and other bookstores. Every so though often he would add bestsellers to his collection, not unlike the ones Noah was unpacking today. He didn't know what they were but based on the density and weight of the books, he could tell they weren't a light read.

With the books carefully stacked in his arms, Noah kicked open the swinging door separating him from the rest of the store. He navigated his way through the young adult section into literary fiction where his coworker Jada was flirting with her boyfriend of the week, who was too enamored to even notice Noah. Jada, on the other hand, glanced at him long enough to make sure he wouldn't say anything, then resumed her dalliance.

I'll say something later, he thought to himself, though the truth was, he probably wouldn't.

Noah neared the paranormal romance

shelves next. The only thing he knew about this genre was that it was populated with lovesick vampires, forlorn werewolves and gregarious ghosts. He wasn't sure what they had to do with romance, but then there were many things he didn't understand, women being the first.

Though he was in his late-twenties, Noah had had only one girlfriend: Sage. Tall, slender, with blonde-brown hair, she was the epitome of beauty. So, he was a little shocked when she asked him out. She did most of the talking through their first, second and third dates. And most of the kissing too. But then she started making innuendoes about his life, his job and his ambitions, or lack thereof. True, he had been employed at the bookstore since high-school, but he was *employed*. Surely that counted for something. And he had gone from stock boy to manager. He had learned a trade. He could pay his rent and put gas in his car. He wasn't lazy or ambitionless, he was content. Was that so bad?

Apparently for Sage, it was; and after two months of dating, she dropped him in favor of someone with 'bigger' goals—her personal trainer. Noah was devastated, but he found solace in the fact that his life could have been worse. How, he wasn't sure, but things could always be much worse, or so the saying went.

With a resigned sigh, Noah readjusted the bestsellers in his arms and continued forward, turning the corner into the fantasy section, another subject he didn't understand. Yes, he could be pragmatic about things, but to live in a world where reality was set aside for the fantastic? It just didn't make sense. What did dragons, dwarves and leather-clad muscle-heads have on flesh and blood?

His thoughts lost on the subject at hand, Noah didn't notice he wasn't alone in the aisle until he was midway through it. It was only then he glanced up and locked eyes with *her*—a voluptuous beauty with copper-colored tresses that bounced as she walked towards him. She had an almond-shaped face with beautiful brown eyes; full, rosy lips; and the most naturally tanned skin he had ever seen. She had been in the store a couple times before, but each time, Noah was otherwise occupied with Bill or a customer. She was striking then, just as she was now, and as she moved closer to him, he found himself captivated by her beauty. There was something so wondrously intoxicating about her, Noah couldn't help but stare. He stopped walking and simply stood in the aisle, waiting as she drew closer to him. Her steps were soft on the carpet, her feet small and dainty. She was shapely, filling every inch of the shorts and long-sleeve t-shirt she was wearing. Her handbag was tucked underneath her arm, while her hips swayed as she approached him.

You should probably move out of her way, he thought to himself, but his brain had ceased communicating to the rest of his body. He couldn't move.

She stopped, mere inches between them, and gazed at him with her lovely brown eyes. Noah could see the freckles dotting her nose. He could smell the lavender on her skin and in her hair. For a moment, he thought to ask her if she needed help, but he was dumbstruck in that department as well.

Without saying a word, she rose up on her tiptoes and leaned into him. A couple of the books slid out of his arms as she held onto him for support, but she neither apologized nor broke eye contact. She simply smiled, then closed her eyes. She leaned further in, knocking more books out of his arms, and gently kissed him.

Noah's heart was thundering so loud in his chest, he was certain she could hear it. It wasn't every day (or ever) that a beautiful woman walked up to him and kissed him, so once again, he was at a loss of what to do or how to react...until she parted her lips. He felt her tongue on his lower lip and it was all the encouragement he needed. He opened his mouth and let his tongue find hers. The books dropped from his arms, and he intuitively filled them with the mystery woman instead.

As their tongues mated, Noah let his hands slide up and down her arms, feeling the warmth of her body beneath his touch. All thought left him as her hands rested on his chest and her body pressed against his. She felt soft in his embrace—warm, inviting, like she belonged there; and in that moment, she did. Noah was never this spontaneous, impulsive or daring, but something about her just felt right.

The woman took his lower lip in her mouth and gently sucked on it. Then she released him and pulled back ever so slowly, opening her eyes as she went. There was a brief flash of vulnerability in them, followed by a glint of mischief. She dropped her arms and took a step back away from him. Noah suddenly felt empty without her. He was missing something he didn't know existed minutes before; and the worst part was that he still couldn't function—he didn't know what to say or do. It seemed she had robbed him of everything but his breath.

The woman bent down to pick up her handbag, which had spilled its contents on the floor, alongside the books. Instinctively,

Noah stooped down with her to help her, but she had already gathered her things. He found himself staring into her eyes instead. She offered him a flirtatious smile then kissed him again, this time quick and playful. She licked her lips, then quickly rose to her feet and started her retreat.

"Noah!" he heard behind him.

Try as he might though, he couldn't pull himself away from the view the mysterious woman was offering him: her lovely backside swinging with every step she took.

"Noah! Noah!"

He gazed over his shoulder briefly to see his coworkers Cass and Jada at the other end of the aisle, wide-eyed and smiling. His face warmed as he imagined what the scene must have looked like to them. Noah turned back to where the woman had been, but she was gone, the door chime announcing her departure as it had her arrival.

"Go after her," Cass exclaimed; and with that command, Noah was seemingly released from whatever trance the woman had him in. With his heart pounding hard once again, he stood up and jumped over the books, running down the aisle towards the door. He didn't know why it didn't occur to him to follow after the woman, but now that he was, he wanted only to catch up to her…though he wasn't sure what he would say once he caught her.

Outside, Noah stopped to look around him. The bookstore was situated in the old downtown area, filled with small shops, restaurants and an urban park. Business was steady enough to keep them all employed, as older adults strolled about, families with little ones went in search of adventure and teenagers loitered…but no woman. Noah ran to the corner and down the cross street, but she wasn't there either.

She was gone.

Disappointed, he returned to the bookstore, his steps slower and heavier. Noah replayed the scene in his head, marveling at the surrealism of it, but also relishing the memory of her kiss. He had always been something of a loner, never finding the time to date (or if he was honest, never finding *a girl* to date). He wasn't especially handsome: dirty brown hair, dull eyes and a lean body. Okay, he was skinny. Skinny and unappealing. So, what was he supposed to make of the woman and her kiss?

The whole thing was just something weird I'll tell my kids about one day, he thought. *If I ever have kids.*

Cass and Jada met him at the door.

"What was that?"

"Who was that?"

"Oh my God, she was gorgeous."

"Did you see her?"

"Damn, she was hot!"

"Who was she?"

"What was that all about?"

"Do you know her?"

"Have you guys dated before? Do you even know each other?"

"I mean, seriously, the way you were sucking each other's faces, right?"

Cass and Jada were twenty-two and nineteen respectively.

Noah shook his head in response—to everything—and continued towards the aisle where he left the books. The women walked with him, Jada's boyfriend not too far behind them.

"Seriously, Noah, who was that?" Cass asked.

"I don't know," he mumbled.

"What's going on?"

The quartet stopped as the bookstore's namesake and their boss, Bill, joined them. He was in his late fifties with a thick midsection and a bald head. He was not a patient man and often talked about closing the store and starting a new business, but he never did. Though he liked Noah, his opinion of young people was very low—they were 'smart-mouthed and mostly lazy' and only lived to aggravate him.

Like today.

"Noah was kissing one of the customers," Jada explained.

Bill glared at him disapprovingly, his eyebrow arched high into his forehead.

"I don't know who she was," Noah argued. He couldn't imagine that fraternizing with potential clients was a fire-able offense, but it didn't hurt to explain himself. "She just came up to me and kissed me."

"They were making out in paranormal romance aisle," Jada added, a broad smile on her face. "Fitting, huh?"

Cass elbowed her, while Noah glowered at his young coworker. Bill seemed to realize then they were not alone. He frowned at Jada's boyfriend and asked, "Who are you?"

Everyone looked to the young man, who shirked back after suddenly becoming the center of attention. He grabbed a book off the shelf and mumbled, "Uhm, I'm here to get a book."

Without a glance in either direction, he wandered off.

Bill said, "Alright girls, back to the front. Noah, clean up," an air of resignation in his voice as though this was something else he should be disappointed with. Then without another word, Bill walked back to his office.

Rather than obey, the young women remained with Noah. As if the questions they had plied him with before weren't enough, Noah knew they were about to unload on him as soon as Bill was out of hearing range. He didn't wait around for the inquisition and moved to do as he was told.

Of course, the girls followed.

"That was kinda romantic, don't you think?" Cass postured out loud, a hint of humor in her voice.

"I don't know," he muttered, wondering at the anonymity of the situation. Then without thinking of the ammunition he would be providing the women, he added, "She's been here a couple times. I've seen her before." He mentally kicked himself when Jada quipped, "Apparently scoping out more than the merchandise."

Noah blushed.

"Well, I think that was romantic," Cass replied, her tone dreamy and lost.

"Why leave then without giving me a name or something? What was that all about?" he asked.

"Aw, Noah's feelings are hurt," Jada mocked, bored with the direction of the conversation. She wasn't always mean-spirited, but she did prefer to be the center of attention.

"Don't listen to her," Cass said, winding

her arm in his. Like the mystery woman, she also had a healthy amount of weight on her and stood just inches shorter than him, but they were two different people. Cass was...well, Cass and the mystery woman? There was something about her that had his brain scrambled. "Jada's just jealous," Cass continued, "You have beautiful women stalking you while she has to put out just for a little attention."

Jada stopped walking and placed her hands on her hips, her mouth open in indignation. But when neither Noah nor Cass gave her the attention she wanted, she dropped her arms and ran up beside them.

"Whatever," Jada muttered. "At least I know a guy's name when I screw him."

Noah could offer no objection to that argument.

"Maybe she's playing hard to get," Cass reasoned.

"It would've been nice then if she could've left me a clue or something," Noah said, as they arrived at the books he dropped earlier. He cringed when he saw them: several covers were creased, pages were folded or torn and a couple of spines were bent out of shape. With a sigh, Noah hunched over and started piling up the books, straightening them up as he went along. One-by-one the stack grew, until there was nothing on the floor…except a piece of paper. He retrieved it and looked it over. It was an old receipt with random things scribbled all over it. It wasn't his, nor was it in the aisle before—the woman must have dropped it.

"Seems she did," Cass said.

Acknowledgements

Thank you to my editor, Jaclyn Lee, whose insight and help with my manuscripts are invaluable. Thank you to my beta readers, who are always willing to read what I write and get back to me on schedule. Thank you to all my fans, for your love, your encouragement…and for buying my stuff. And as always, thank you to my wonderful husband and family, for loving me.

About the Author

Ruth E. Griffin could draw pictures before she could put sentences together. Eventually, though, she figured out how to do both and is now the author of several books (fiction and non-fiction) which center on women's experiences. She still designs but focuses all her free time on writing. Ruth currently lives in North Carolina with her husband and three children. Her work is available at major online bookstores, while new book release/event information can be found at www.ruthegriffin.com. Email her at ruthegriffin@outlook.com.